RIDE OF COURAGE

TREASURED HORSES COLLECTION™

titles in Large-Print Editions:

RIDE OF COURAGE

*The story of a spirited Arabian horse
and the daring girl who rides him*

Written by **Deborah Felder**
Illustrated by **Sandy Rabinowitz**
Cover Illustration by **Christa Keiffer**
Developed by Nancy Hall, Inc.

Gareth Stevens Publishing
MILWAUKEE

For a free color catalog describing Gareth Stevens' list of high-quality books and multimedia programs, call 1-800-542-2595 (USA) or 1-800-461-9120 (Canada). Gareth Stevens Publishing's Fax: (414) 225-0377.

Library of Congress Cataloging-in-Publication Data

Felder, Deborah G.
  Ride of courage / written by Deborah Felder; illustrated by Sandy Rabinowitz; cover illustration by Christa Keiffer.
      p. cm.
  Originally published: Dyersville, Iowa: Ertl Co., 1996.
  (Treasured horses collection)
  Summary: In 1781, twelve-year-old Molly Randall, living with her family in Yorktown, Virginia, finds her courage tested when she must ride a powerful Arabian horse to get help for a neighbor about to be executed for treason by the British.
      ISBN 0-8368-2280-3 (lib. bdg.)
      1. Virginia—History—Revolution, 1775-1783—Juvenile fiction.
  [1. Virginia—History—Revolution, 1775-1783—Fiction.
  2. United States—History—Revolution, 1775-1783—Fiction.
  3. Arabian horse—Fiction. 4. Horses—Fiction.] I. Rabinowitz, Sandy, ill. II. Title. III. Series: Treasured horses collection.
  PZ7.F3356Ri   1999
  [Fic]—dc21   98-46304

This edition first published in 1999 by
Gareth Stevens Publishing
1555 North RiverCenter Drive, Suite 201
Milwaukee, Wisconsin 53212 USA

Printed in the United States of America

1 2 3 4 5 6 7 8 9 03 02 01 00 99

CONTENTS

CHAPTER ONE

At the Blacksmith's Forge

"Molly! Molly Randall! Goodness, where *is* that child?"

It was a warm September day in Yorktown, Virginia. The year was 1781. Molly Randall lay on her bed in the room she shared with her older sister. Molly lay on her stomach, her chin propped up in her hands. She was gazing dreamily out at the meadow where the family's small chestnut mare, Flora, was grazing.

Flora was twelve years old, the same age as Molly. She was fun to ride and Molly loved her very much. But Molly sometimes wondered what it would be like

to ride a bigger and more powerful horse. She began to imagine herself galloping across the meadow on Sultan, the beautiful Arabian gelding owned by Richard Butler, a wealthy horse breeder. Molly was just about to jump Sultan over the gate and into the yard, when she felt a tap on her shoulder. She turned to see her fifteen-year-old sister, Anne, standing by the bed, her hands on her hips and an impatient look on her face.

"So here you are," Anne said in an annoyed tone. "It's five-thirty. Ma is waiting for you in the kitchen. It's your turn to take the supper basket out to Pa and Ethan, remember?"

Molly and Anne's father, John, was the town blacksmith. Their seventeen-year-old brother, Ethan, worked at the forge alongside his father. The Randalls had shared their midday meal together in the house. But because Molly's father and brother worked until dusk in the summer, they usually ate their supper outside near the forge.

"All right, I'm going," Molly told her sister. She scrambled off the bed and hurried out of the room.

The Randalls' house had four rooms. Besides Molly and Anne's bedroom, there was also a bedroom for their parents. Ethan slept in a small loft above the main room. The main room was furnished very simply, with a polished wood table and chairs, two rocking chairs, and a wooden bench. In the middle of the room was a wood-burning stove that warmed the bedrooms and Ethan's loft in winter.

In the kitchen, Molly's mother, Caroline, was standing over the large pine work table placing a jug of cider in a basket.

"I'm sorry, Ma," Molly said. "I forgot that I was supposed to bring Pa and Ethan their supper today. I was just . . ."

"Daydreaming as usual, " her mother finished as she tucked a cloth into the sides of the basket. She turned to face her daughter. "It's nice to have daydreams, Molly," she added. "But you have chores to do, too, just like the rest of us."

"The only chore Molly ever remembers to do is to take care of Flora," Anne said as she stepped into the kitchen. She was carrying a pail full of milk from the Randalls' cow, Daisy.

"That's not true," Molly said hotly. "I brought the eggs in from the henhouse this morning. I helped Ma make apple jelly this afternoon. And I milked Daisy yesterday, didn't I?"

"Yes, but then you went running down to the river to look at an English ship. You left the milk pail right behind Daisy's legs and she knocked it over," Anne

shot back. Molly opened her mouth to answer her
sister back, but before she could say anything, her
mother said firmly, "That's enough, girls. Molly, here's
the basket. There's extra ham, cheese, and bread, so
you can share Pa and Ethan's supper. But don't forget
to bring the basket back afterwards."

Molly took the basket from her mother. "I won't
forget, Ma, I promise," she said with a sigh.

Why does Ma always treat me like a baby, Molly
thought as she left the house and began walking the
few yards to the forge. Just because I have to be
reminded to do my chores sometimes? What about the
other day, when Anne forgot to bring the washing
inside and it began to rain?

Molly walked along, looking down at the ground.
"It just isn't fair, " she muttered, kicking at a stone
with her buckled shoe.

"What isn't fair?" Molly suddenly heard a booming
voice say. She raised her head and saw Josiah
Thomas, the ironmonger, grinning at her from the
doorway of the forge. He was so tall, his head nearly
touched the top of the doorway, and so heavyset that
Molly could barely see behind him into the forge. But
she could hear the clanging sound of a hammer
beating a horseshoe into shape and a voice talking in
soothing tones to a horse, and she knew that her

father and brother were hard at work.

Molly didn't answer Mr. Thomas's question. Instead, she asked eagerly, "Did you bring Marigold over to be shod? May I see her?"

"Of course you may," Mr. Thomas said cheerfully. "But I'd wait until your pa and Ethan are finished with her. She's been acting a little skittish lately."

Molly placed the supper basket on the bench in front of the forge and walked to the doorway of the building. Mr. Thomas stepped aside to let her pass, then followed her inside.

In the middle of the large room stood Marigold. She was a pretty bay mare with a white star on her forehead and white stockings. Molly's brother, Ethan, was holding her by the halter and stroking her satiny neck. John Randall was gently holding one of Marigold's hind legs between his legs and firmly tapping a horsehoe into the bottom of her hoof. Ethan's hound, Jack, was snuffling around the floor of the forge looking for bits of hoof to chew on.

Molly's father and brother were dressed alike, in linen breeches and white shirts. Leather aprons protected their clothes. Their long, curly light-brown hair, the same color as Molly's, was tied back with black ribbons.

Ethan smiled at his sister. "I hope you brought a

lot of supper for us," he said. "I'm starved!"

Molly nodded absently. She was busy watching her father as he finished nailing on the shoe and moved around the mare to start on her other hoof. When he raised her leg, Marigold tossed her head and snorted. Then she began to step backward and forward nervously.

"Whoa, Marigold," Ethan said softly, stroking the mare's neck. "Whoa, girl. Nobody's going to hurt you." After several seconds, the mare calmed down.

"I knew she'd be skittish," Josiah Thomas said. "It's because of all those redcoats swarming around. Yorktown was a nice, quiet town before they came here."

Without looking up from his work, Molly's father said quietly, "None of us like having the redcoats in Yorktown, Josiah."

"Still, I have to admit that they're good for business," Mr. Thomas said with a laugh. "They've bought a lot of tools from me."

Molly saw her brother's face darken with anger at the ironmonger's words. She understood why. For six years, American colonists had been fighting British soldiers to gain independence from England. The British soldiers were nicknamed "redcoats" because of the red jackets they wore. There had been an army of redcoats in Yorktown since August.

Most of the colonists in Yorktown, like the Randalls, were patriots loyal to the American cause. But a few shopkeepers and craftspeople like Josiah Thomas were willing to do business with the redcoats even though they insisted that they were patriots. And that made Ethan mad.

Molly suddenly thought of something. "Pa, why haven't the redcoats brought their horses here to be shod?" she asked.

"The British army has its own blacksmith," her father replied. "Anyway, we don't need their business."

"Nor do we want it," Ethan said scornfully. "We're not traitors."

Molly glanced over to see if Josiah Thomas had heard what Ethan had said. But Mr. Thomas had gone outside. She looked around the forge. Ever since she was a tiny child, she had loved being here with the horses and Pa and her brother. She had watched Pa and Ethan carefully in the hope that someday they would let her help them. Maybe today was the day.

"Can I help you and Ethan finish shoeing Marigold, Pa?" Molly asked.

Ethan laughed. "Don't be silly, Molly. This is man's work, not work for little girls like you."

"Well, I could at least hold on to Marigold's halter,

like you're doing," Molly argued. "I know how to handle her and talk to her. She and I are old friends."

Ethan shook his head. "She's much too skittish today."

"Ethan's right, " Pa said, straightening up. "Blacksmithing can be dangerous work. You're too young to help. Maybe in a few years, but not now." He came over to Molly and put his arm around her shoulders. "Why don't you set up our supper under the willow tree?" he suggested. "Ethan and I will be out in a few minutes, and then we'll have a picnic."

Molly shrugged off her father's arm and marched out of the forge. She snatched up the supper basket and headed over to the willow tree. Under the tree was a rough wooden table and two benches built by her father. Molly set the basket on the table and began to unpack it. "I'll show them," she muttered. "I can do anything Ethan can do. Pa just won't let me try." She gazed off into the distance and tried hard to think of how she could show her family that she was responsible. But try as she might, she couldn't think of anything.

Just then, Molly heard a long, high-pitched neigh coming from the direction of the road. She turned to look, and her eyes lit up. Coming down the road toward the forge were Richard Butler and Sultan. Molly grinned at the sight of the beautiful Arabian. His dapple-gray coat gleamed in the bright sunshine, his gray-and-white tail waved proudly, and he held his head high. Molly liked all the horses that came to the forge, but Sultan was special.

Molly liked Mr. Butler, too, even though she knew he was a Tory. Tories were Americans who had stayed loyal to England. Mr. Butler and his wife, Julia, lived on a farm called Brookfield, which was a few miles outside of Yorktown. There, Mr. Butler bred Arabian horses. Molly had never seen Mr. Butler's other Arabians, but she was sure none of them were as beautiful as Sultan.

Suddenly, Molly realized that Mr. Butler was not alone. Riding behind him were two redcoats on horseback. She heard Josiah Thomas's deep laugh and turned to see the ironmonger step out of the forge, followed by her father, brother, and Jack. Ethan was leading Marigold out the door. Mr. Thomas counted out some coins into John Randall's hand, clapped him on the shoulder, and took Marigold's lead line from Ethan. Then he began leading Marigold toward the town.

Talking and laughing, Pa and Ethan started walking toward Molly. Then they stopped in their tracks and stared at the riders approaching the forge.

Molly hurried over to her father.

"Why is Mr. Butler coming here with two redcoats?" she asked. "You said the redcoats had their own blacksmith."

Her father put his arm around her and held her close. "Maybe they won't stop here," he murmured. "They may just be riding into town."

A moment later, Richard Butler and the two redcoats turned their horses onto the short lane that led from the road to the Randalls' forge.

Molly looked up at her father. He was pale and there was a worried expression on his face. All at once she remembered that only yesterday, one of their neighbors had been arrested by the redcoats as a patriot spy. He was a very old man who walked with a cane, but he had still been arrested.

The happiness Molly had been feeling at the thought of seeing Sultan turned to fear. Richard Butler knew her father and brother were patriots. Was he bringing the redcoats to the forge to arrest them?

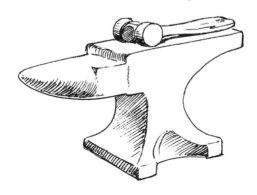

Sultan

Molly watched Richard Butler and the redcoats ride toward them. She had often seen redcoats in the town and riding up and down the main road. But now, for the first time, they were on the Randalls' property.

The men brought their horses to a stop and dismounted. They began walking the horses over to where the Randalls were standing. Molly heard her father take a deep breath.

"What are you going to do, Pa?" she whispered.

"I'm going to act as if nothing is wrong," Pa said evenly. "And I would like you and Ethan to act the same way." Without hesitating, he started toward the three men, a smile on his face.

"Good evening, gentlemen," Molly heard him say in a pleasant tone. "What can I do for you? Mr. Butler, have you been riding Sultan so hard that he needs to be shod again?"

Richard Butler removed his three-cornered hat and smiled back at John Randall. Mr. Butler was a tall, handsome man in his mid-forties. He had long, black hair that was graying at the temples, and he was wearing a riding jacket, breeches, and black leather boots.

Mr. Butler gave Sultan an affectionate pat and shook his head. "Sultan's shoes are in fine shape, thanks to you, Mr. Randall," he said. "I happened to be riding into town on some business, when I came upon these officers. They have just arrived in Yorktown, and they are looking for a barn where they can stable their horses."

Molly breathed a sigh of relief. So the redcoats hadn't come here to arrest Pa and Ethan after all! She turned to see if her brother was as relieved as she was. But Ethan had disappeared.

Molly looked around the yard. After a moment, she saw him. He had just left the house and was striding toward them. Molly's eyes widened in surprise when she saw that he was carrying a musket.

Molly ran over to her brother. "What are you doing with that musket?" she asked anxiously. "You're not going to *shoot* the redcoats, are you, Ethan?"

Ethan didn't look at his sister. He just kept on walking, his head held high, and his eyes fixed on the redcoats standing several yards away. "No," he said in a low voice. "But if there's going to be any trouble, I want to be ready to fight."

Molly had to jog along next to her brother to keep up with his long stride. "But there isn't going to be any trouble," she said breathlessly. "The redcoats came here to ask us if we'll take care of their horses. Mr. Butler just said so."

By now, they had reached the men. John Randall frowned at his son and held out his hand. "We have no need of a musket, Ethan," he said quietly. "Give it to me."

Ethan hesitated for a moment. Then he handed the gun to his father. Without taking his eyes off his son, John Randall nodded toward the two officers and said, "These officers are Captain Foster and Lieutenant Hayden. I have agreed to let them stable their horses in the two empty stalls of our barn."

Ethan looked at his father in alarm. Then the expression on his face changed. He scowled at the officers and said coldly, "My father made a mistake.

We would never take care of horses that belong to the enemy. We're patriots!"

"Mind your manners, Ethan," snapped his father. "Go and prepare the stalls. And be sure to spread fresh straw on the floor."

Without another word, Ethan turned and stomped off toward the barn.

"Your son's a bit of a hothead, sir," Captain Foster said, speaking for the first time.

The captain was a tall, thin man with red hair. Lieutenant Hayden was short and stocky, and he had blond hair. Molly noticed that the jackets and breeches of both officers were splattered with mud.

"Ethan is young, and he's a patriot," Molly's father said shortly. "As are most of us who live in Yorktown. And now, why don't you gentlemen take your horses over to the barn."

"Patriot or no, we are much obliged to you," Lieutenant Hayden said stiffly.

Molly watched Lieutenant Hayden and Captain Foster lead their horses in the direction of the barn. She had been a little surprised when her father had agreed to help the redcoats. But when she looked at the lieutenant's black gelding and the captain's white mare, she understood why. The horses were thin, their coats were dull, and their tails drooped. They hung their heads as if they were very tired. Molly knew that Pa loved horses as much as she did. He couldn't stand to see them suffer. He would never turn away a horse that needed help.

Pa turned to follow the captain and the lieutenant. But before he did, Molly spotted the look that passed between him and Richard Butler. It was almost as if they were sharing a secret. Something mysterious was going on. But what?

"Well, Molly, aren't you going to say hello to Sultan?" she heard Richard Butler ask. "Or did you forget that he was here in all the excitement?" he added teasingly.

"No, sir, I didn't forget," Molly replied shyly, stepping up to Sultan. The Arabian greeted her with a low, soft nicker. Reaching out a hand, Molly began to stroke his velvety neck. "Hello, Sultan," she said softly. Sultan stood quietly, his neck arched and his ears pricked forward. "Sultan likes you," Mr. Butler said. "He's very high-spirited, and young people often make him skittish. But I've watched you with Sultan when I've brought him here to be shod. You know exactly how to handle him."

Molly glowed with pleasure at Mr. Butler's compliment. "Sultan's the most beautiful horse in Virginia," she said. "No, that's wrong. He's the most

beautiful horse in the whole thirteen American
colonies!"

At that, Sultan shook his head up and down
several times, rippling his thick, white mane.

"Sultan seems to agree with you," Mr. Butler said
with a laugh. "I'm glad you think he's beautiful. But
you haven't seen all the other Arabians at Brookfield.
And I've heard that General George Washington's
Arabian mare, Magnolia, is very pretty. Still, Sultan *is*
special."

He pulled a watch from his jacket pocket and
glanced at it. "I'd better be on my way," he said,
replacing the watch. Molly reluctantly stepped away
from Sultan so that Mr. Butler could draw the reins
over the Arabian's head. Mr. Butler placed his foot in
the stirrup on Sultan's left side and swung easily into
the saddle. Eager to be off, Sultan began to prance
restlessly back and forth.

"Whoa, boy," Mr. Butler said, reaching down to pat
Sultan's neck. When Sultan had calmed down, Mr.
Butler looked over at Molly. "Why don't you come out
to Brookfield tomorrow afternoon, if your mother and
father can spare you? Mrs. Butler wants to show you
the new foal that was born this morning. And you
can take Sultan for a ride, too, if you'd like."

When Mr. Butler came to the forge, he often

invited Molly to ride Sultan. And every time he did, Molly said no. She loved Sultan, but she also knew that riding him wouldn't be as easy as riding Flora. The mare was a small horse, only fourteen hands high, and easy to control. But Sultan was more than a hand higher than Flora and much more powerful and spirited.

Molly gazed longingly at Sultan. The memory of her daydream about riding him across the meadow came back to her. Then the daydream faded, and she shook her head with regret.

"I don't think I can ride Sultan, Mr. Butler," she said with a sigh. "Not yet, anyway."

Mr. Butler nodded. "I understand. When you're ready, let me know."

Just then, Molly's father came up to them. "I've asked Molly out to Brookfield Farm tomorrow to see the new foal," Mr. Butler told him. "Will that be all right with you, Mr. Randall? I'll send over my stable boy Thomas to escort her." Molly's father nodded. "As long as you're back by five o'clock, Molly, you may go."

"Thank you, Pa!" Molly cried, throwing her arms around her father.

"I'll have Thomas call for you at two o'clock, Molly," Mr. Butler said. With that, he touched his boots lightly to Sultan's sides, turned the Arabian toward the lane, and urged him into a canter.

"I wonder," John Randall murmured, stroking his chin thoughtfully.

Molly, her eyes shining, had been watching Sultan canter gracefully down the road toward the town. Now she turned to her father and asked, "What do you wonder, Pa?"

"Oh, nothing," Pa said hastily. He ruffled Molly's brown curls. "Well, daughter, I think it's time we had our supper, don't you?"

Molly grinned and nodded. All of a sudden, she felt very hungry.

As they were walking over to the table under the willow tree, Molly remembered the two British officers. "What happened to the redcoats, Pa?" she asked. "Are they still here?"

Pa shook his head and pointed to the road. Molly looked over to where her father was pointing and saw Captain Foster and Lieutenant Hayden trudging wearily down the road toward the town.

"They're on their way to General Cornwallis's headquarters," Pa explained. "They need to report to him and to find out where the rest of the soldiers in their regiment are staying."

Molly knew that General Cornwallis was the commanding officer of the British troops in Yorktown.

She had once seen him riding down the road at the head of a long double line of British soldiers. He had been dressed in a fancy uniform, and his powdered hair was carefully styled. Molly remembered the cold, haughty expression on his face.

Molly and her father sat at the table. She had just finished unwrapping the cloth-covered packets of ham and cheese, when she saw her brother coming toward them. Ethan sat on the bench next to Molly and said abruptly, "I rubbed down the horses. The redcoats had nosebags with them, so I gave the horses some oats and bran, too."

"Good," said Pa with an approving nod. "Now, why don't you join us and have some supper?"

Ethan stared at the food. Then he shook his head and muttered, "I'm not hungry anymore. I'm going down to the river." He stood up, rounded the table, and walked away.

"I guess Ethan is still upset because you agreed to take care of the redcoats' horses," Molly said between bites. "But you had to take them, Pa. They look so thin and tired. What happened to them? Did those redcoats treat them badly?"

"Not on purpose, Molly," Pa answered. "But you have to remember that they're army horses. Their job is to carry soldiers into battle. I suspect that Captain

27

Foster and Lieutenant Hayden became trapped near the battlefield after the British troops were beaten south by French and German troops who are on our side. They were desperate to get back to Yorktown and had little time to think of their horses.

He wiped his mouth on his napkin, and stood up. "I'm going to check on the horses. Then I need to go into town on an errand. I won't be back until late. If you see Ethan, ask him to straighten up the forge."

"Yes, Pa," Molly replied. She picked up the basket and started for the house. As she walked, she saw that the sun was beginning to sink lower in the sky. "I'd better bring Flora in," she said to herself. "She needs her supper, too."

When Molly reached the house, her mother and Anne were sitting down at the table having their supper.

"Pa told us what happened with the redcoats and Ethan," Anne said. "I'm glad I don't have to take care of their horses."

"That's just because you don't like horses," Molly retorted as she picked an apple out of the basket and put it in her pocket. "Well, I love horses, and I'll be happy to look after them." With that, Molly headed out to the barn.

When she got there, she lifted Flora's halter and

lead rope off the hook outside her stall. She hurried out of the barn and began to run toward the meadow. She reached the fence that ran all the way around the meadow and stopped short, unable to believe her eyes. The gate was wide open and Flora was nowhere in sight!

Where Is Flora?

"**F**lora!" Molly called out. The mare usually trotted up to Molly when she heard her name. But this time, there was no answering whinny. And no Flora.

What could have happened to her? Molly wondered desperately. Molly, Ethan, and Anne all knew how important it was to keep the gate closed because of Daisy. The cow had a habit of wandering into Ma's vegetable garden if anyone left the gate open, even for a short time.

Molly had a terrible thought. The black gelding and the white mare wouldn't be ready to ride for several days. What if one of those redcoats had seen Flora and decided to steal her?

Just then, Molly saw Ethan walking toward her from the direction of the river. Molly ran over to him.

"Pa sent you to get me, didn't he?" Ethan said with a scowl. "He probably wants me to get back to work. That's all I'm good for, working in the forge and taking care of redcoats' horses. He doesn't seem to care that there's a war going on, and . . ."

"Oh, Ethan, something terrible has happened," Molly broke in. "Flora's missing!"

"What!" Ethan exclaimed. "But how did she . . . ?" He looked over at the gate, and his face turned red with embarrassment. "I guess I forgot to close the gate when I went down to the river."

"Now Flora is gone," Molly said in a trembling voice full of tears.

Ethan put his arm around his sister. "I'm sorry, Molly. But don't worry, we'll find her."

Molly brushed the tears from her eyes. "Let's look in the barn first. Maybe Flora wandered back there."

The two of them hurried off toward the barn. When they passed the house and came to the water trough, Molly suddenly had an idea of where Flora might be.

"Keep looking!" she shouted to her brother. Then, still carrying Flora's halter and lead rope, she headed for the lane that led to the road.

When Molly got to the road, she began walking away from the town, in the direction of the countryside. She had remembered where Flora had gone the first time she escaped from the meadow. Molly and her father found the mare at the water trough belonging to Andrew Graham, a farmer who lived a little more than a mile up the road.

Molly walked as quickly as she could. She had covered about one-quarter of the distance, when she suddenly stopped in her tracks. Last week, Graham's farm had been taken over by redcoats. Andrew Graham and his family had been ordered to leave the farm and find somewhere else to live.

Molly bit her lip as she stood staring at the stretch of road before her. She was scared at the thought of facing all those redcoats at Graham's farm. Would they help her? Or would they want to keep Flora?

"I have to find Flora," she told herself. But, somehow, she couldn't make herself move forward.

Then she heard the clippity-clopping sound of a cantering horse behind her. Was it a redcoat? Molly whirled around in terror, then relaxed as she saw who was riding toward her. It was Richard Butler on Sultan. Mr. Butler held an unlit lantern in one hand.

He slowed Sultan to a stop and reined him in beside Molly. He looked down at Molly in surprise. "Is something wrong? You look worried."

"Flora's missing," Molly explained. "I think she's at Graham's farm. But there are redcoats at the farm now, and I'm afraid to go there."

Mr. Butler dismounted. He said gently, "Then we'll go to Graham's farm together. If Flora is there, we'll get her back, never fear."

Mr. Butler handed Sultan's reins to her. "Hold these while I make the stirrups shorter," he told her. "You'll have to ride Sultan while I lead him."

Molly took the reins, holding them just tightly enough to show Sultan that she was in control. With mounting fear mingled with excitement, she watched Mr. Butler release the stirrup bars and adjust the stirrups to a shorter length. Soon she would be sitting in the saddle on the proud Arabian. It was a moment she had both feared and longed for.

"There," Mr. Butler said finally. "We're ready." He turned, leaned over a little, and laced his fingers together so that his hands formed a cup.

Molly took a deep breath. Swallowing her fear, she placed the reins on the pommel of the saddle and put her left foot into Mr. Butler's hands. Instantly, she felt her body being lifted up and she swung her right leg over Sultan's back. The horse began to prance as Molly struggled to right herself in the saddle.

Instinctively, she grabbed hold of the martingale strap. Mr. Butler took the reins from her and patted Sultan's neck. "Good boy," he said soothingly. "Calm down now." Sultan immediately stopped prancing.

Molly settled herself in the saddle and placed her other foot in the stirrup. "Ready?" Mr. Butler asked with an encouraging smile. Molly gulped and nodded. "I think so," she replied in a small voice.

"Right," said Mr. Butler. "Let's go."

He tugged on the reins slightly, and Sultan moved forward. Despite her fear of riding Sultan, and her worry over Flora and facing redcoats, Molly soon found that she was moving in rhythm with the Arabian. She began to relax and enjoy the exciting feeling of riding the powerful horse.

The sun was beginning to set when Molly, Mr. Butler, and Sultan reached Graham's farm. As they entered the farmyard, Molly saw redcoats everywhere. Most were sitting in front of campfires eating and talking. Some were leading horses to the barn. Still others were going in or out of the farmhouse.

Mr. Butler helped Molly down off Sultan. She scanned the farmyard eagerly, hoping to spot Flora. A moment later, she broke into a smile. "There she is," Molly cried, pointing to the water trough that stood between the barn and the farmhouse.

Molly raced toward the water trough. As she did, she ran straight into a group of redcoats who had stopped in front of the water trough, and were talking and laughing with one another.

In her haste to reach Flora, Molly forgot to be afraid of the soldiers."Excuse me, gentlemen," she said in a firm voice. "Could you let me through, please?"

The soldiers stopped talking to stare at her. One of them shrugged and said, "Certainly, young lady." He and the other soldiers stepped aside to let Molly pass.

Molly rushed over to Flora, reaching her just as the little mare was raising her head from the water trough. When she saw Molly, she nickered softly. Molly threw her arms around Flora's neck and buried her face in the mare's chestnut-colored mane.

"Oh, Flora, I'm so glad I found you," Molly said in a muffled voice.

"So Flora is her name, is it?" she heard a voice say with a chuckle. "I was wondering about that."

Molly jerked up her head. In the twilight, she could barely make out the figure of a grizzled old soldier. He was sitting comfortably on a pile of sandbags near the water trough, puffing on a long-stemmed clay pipe.

The old soldier got to his feet and stepped over to Molly and Flora. "It was I who spotted your Flora trotting down the road," he told her. "I managed to catch her and bring her into the farmyard for a bit of supper and a drink."

"Thank you, sir, for taking care of Flora."

He patted the horses's neck. "She's a pretty little mare, your Flora. She reminds me of a mare I had back home."

Molly thought the old soldier sounded sad when he mentioned home. Was he homesick for his country?

He started for his pile of sandbags again, then turned and added in a serious tone, "But I'll be giving you a piece of advice before you go, young lady. Don't let Flora loose again. The next time she finds her way here, one of our other soldiers might want to keep her. We're a bit short of horses here."

Molly felt a chill go up her spine at his words. She quickly slipped Flora's halter over her head, snapped the lead rope into place, and led the mare away. She followed Mr. Butler and Sultan through the farmyard, all the while keeping a firm hold on Flora's rope. She was afraid that at any moment, a redcoat might come up to them and try to snatch Flora away.

Night had fallen when Molly at last reached home. She saw her mother, sister, and brother rushing toward her and Mr. Butler. Ethan was carrying a lantern to light the way.

She ran up to her mother and hugged her tightly.

"Thank goodness you're safe," Ma said in a relieved tone.

"Where did you go?" Ethan wanted to know. "I looked everywhere for you."

Molly told them what had happened.

Molly's mother turned to Richard Butler and smiled graciously. "Mr. Butler, thank you for bringing my daughter home safely. She should have had sense enough not to go off without telling us. I'm glad you were there to look after her."

"I'm glad I was there, too, Ma'am," Mr. Butler said with a smile. He hoisted himself up onto Sultan's back. "And now, if you'll excuse me, I'd better be on my way home, or my wife will begin to worry about me."

He was about to turn Sultan toward the lane, when Molly cried, "Wait!" She ran up to Mr. Butler and Sultan. "Thank you for helping me find Flora," she said to Mr. Butler. Then she put her arms around Sultan's neck. "And thank you, Sultan, for letting me ride you," she whispered.

She stepped back and waved as Mr. Butler rode off down the lane.

Molly's Strange Visit

Molly woke to the sound of clanging pans in the kitchen the next morning. She yawned and rolled over. She saw that her sister's bed was empty. She's already up and dressed, and helping Ma in the kitchen, Molly thought sleepily. That figures.

She looked out the window. The sky was blue and the sun was shining brightly, a perfect day for her visit to Brookfield Farm.

Molly got out of bed and dressed. Then she straightened the sheets on her bed, pulled up the quilt, and plumped up the pillow. "That's one chore Ma or Anne won't have to remind me to do," Molly said with a satisfied look at the neatly made bed.

She left the room and walked out to the kitchen. Her mother was lifting a heavy frying pan full of cornbread out of the fireplace. Anne was setting a platter of bacon on the table. Pa and Ethan were already at work in the forge.

"Good morning, dear," Ma said cheerfully as she placed the pan of cornbread on the table and took her place at one end of the table. Anne sat opposite Molly.

"Is Thomas Cole really coming over to take you to the Butlers'?" Anne asked Molly.

Molly looked at her sister. Anne's cheeks were pink and she had an eager expression on her face. Molly knew why.

"Yes, he is," she said. "But I can't understand why you like him. He's so tall and skinny."

"He is not!" Anne protested. "He's good-looking and very nice."

"Finish your breakfast, girls," Ma said quietly. "There's work to be done. Molly, your father would like you to take care of the officers' horses. He said to tell you that the black gelding's name is Pepper and the white mare is called Sweetbriar."

Molly quickly swallowed the last bit of breakfast. Then she jumped up from her chair and asked eagerly, "May I see to the horses now, Ma?"

"Yes, you may," her mother replied. "But don't you

think it would be a good idea for you to put your shoes and stockings on first?"

Molly looked down at her bare legs and feet. Anne passed by with the breakfast plates and said with a smirk, "You'd forget your head if it weren't attached."

Molly waited until her mother's back was turned. Then she made a face at her sister and hurried out of the kitchen. After she had pulled on her stockings and put on her buckled shoes, she ran out to the barn. She grabbed three nosebags that hung on the wall and took them over to a large barrel standing by the hayloft. She removed the top of the barrel and scooped oats and bran into the nosebags.

Molly stepped into Flora's stall and gave the mare a hug and a kiss. Then she hung one of the nosebags over her head. "Have a good breakfast, girl," she said, patting Flora's neck. "You deserve it, even if you did cause us all a lot of trouble yesterday!"

She stepped into Sweetbriar's stall next. The thin white mare turned her head and nickered. She sniffed eagerly at the nosebag. "I know you and Pepper are hungry," Molly said in a soothing voice as she stroked Sweetbriar. "Don't worry, you'll both get plenty to eat while you're here."

After the horses had eaten, Molly brushed them down carefully until their coats shone. Then she led them outside for a drink of water and turned them loose in the meadow, where Daisy was already grazing peacefully. Molly grinned with pleasure when she saw Flora and Sweetbriar touch noses.

Next, Molly cleaned out the horses' stalls and put down fresh straw. By the time she had finished all her chores, she was hot and sticky, and her arms ached from using the pitchfork and pushing the heavy wheelbarrow.

"I need to wash up," she said to herself, wiping her hand across her sweaty forehead. "Ma will be calling us in for dinner soon."

She trudged over to the well near the house. Her father and brother were already there. Ethan was pulling up a big bucket of cool water.

After Molly had washed up, she followed Pa and Ethan into the kitchen, where her mother and Anne were setting platters of fried ham, sweet potatoes, and cornbread on the table.

"Well, Molly," Pa said as he sat down. "How did you like taking care of three horses instead of just one?"

"It was hard work," Molly admitted, taking some ham from the platter. "But it was fun, too. I think Pepper and Sweetbriar really like it here. I wish we could keep them."

"So do I," Pa said with an understanding smile.

When dinner was over, Molly helped her mother and sister clear the table. Then she ran into her room to change her stockings and put on her best dress. The dress was made of homespun linen, like her two everyday dresses, but Ma had dyed the dress until it had turned a rich brown color. There were white cotton frills at the ends of the elbow-length sleeves and a long, snowy white linen collar that tied in front of Molly's bodice. A straw hat that tied under Molly's chin completed her outfit.

After she was dressed, Molly hurried outside to get Flora and saddle her up. As soon as she had hoisted herself into the saddle, Thomas Cole came riding into the yard on a strawberry roan mare. When he saw Molly dressed in her best clothes, he grinned and said, "Why, Molly, how fine you look today. Shall we be on our way?"

Molly smiled at the compliment. Then she turned Flora toward the lane and urged the mare into a canter. The two cantered along in silence. When they reached Brookfield Farm, they turned into a long, curving drive of carefully raked sand and pebbles. And up ahead was the largest house Molly had ever seen. It was white and there were big columns on the front porch. Surrounding the house were large oaks, graceful willow trees, and well-kept gardens. To the right of the house stood the stable, a long, whitewashed building.

After rounding a flower bed with a fountain in the middle, they came to the house. Standing on the front step was Julia Butler. She was a tall, beautiful woman, with black hair piled high on her head and one thick curl falling on her slim neck. The skirts of her elegant silk dress rustled as she stepped off the porch to greet Molly.

Molly slid down off Flora and handed the reins to Thomas. Then, remembering her manners, she curtsied to Mrs. Butler and said, "Good day, ma'am."

Mrs. Butler kissed Molly's cheek. "I am so glad you could come out to see us, Molly," she said, her dark blue eyes sparkling. "Now what will it be first? Would you like a glass of cider? Or would you like to see the new foal?"

"I'd like to visit the foal, ma'am," Molly said shyly. Picking up her skirts, Mrs. Butler led the way over to the stable. Inside the stable, to the right, was a large fenced-in area covered with straw. Standing there was a beautiful light gray Arabian mare with a white mane and tail. She was nuzzling a pure black foal that danced back and forth next to her on its long, wobbly legs.

"Oh," Molly said breathlessly. "It's beautiful. Is it a boy or a girl?"

"A girl—a filly," Julia Butler told her. "And she's very special, too. It's rare for Arabians to be born pure black. In fact, she's so special, we've named her Banat er Rih. In the Arabic language, it means 'Daughter of the Wind'."

"I like that name," Molly said with a smile, as she watched little Banat begin nursing from her mother.

"I'm sorry Richard can't come with us," Mrs. Butler said when they had left the stable and were walking over to the pasture. "He's entertaining a group of British officers at the house this afternoon."

Her words reminded Molly that Mr. and Mrs. Butler were Tories. But she didn't want to think about that right now. All she wanted to do was to see Sultan.

When they reached the pasture, Molly stepped up to the lower bar of the fence, rested her elbows on the top bar, and gazed out over the grassy field. She counted eight horses in the pasture, including Sultan. A few of the Arabians were stretched out on the ground, relaxing, while others were grazing. Molly grinned at the sight of Sultan and a chestnut gelding galloping together wild and free across the pasture.

They stood watching the horses for awhile. Then Mrs. Butler put her arm around Molly and said, "I think it's time we had some refreshments."

"Yes, ma'am," Molly said, stepping down from the fence. She took one last look at Sultan, who was running at the end of the pasture. Then she followed her hostess to a porch at the side of the house. Through the open double doors leading to the inside of the house, Molly could hears the sounds of talk and laughter. She took off her hat and placed it on the floor beside her. Then she glanced into the room and saw Richard Butler standing near the doorway with a group of red-coated officers.

Molly had just finished her cider when Mr. Butler came walking onto the porch. He greeted Molly with a smile, then said, "It's after four o'clock. I promised your father I'd have you back home by five, remember?"

Molly nodded. She put her glass on the tray and stood up. Mrs. Butler stood up, too.

"I need to get back to my guests," Mr. Butler said to Molly in a loud voice. "But before I do, I want to give you something for your father." He held out a folded-up piece of paper. In an even louder voice, he added, "It's a note thanking him for taking such good care of Sultan yesterday."

Puzzled, Molly took the paper from Mr. Butler and put it in her pocket. She knew that nothing had been wrong with Sultan yesterday. What did Mr. Butler mean? And why was he talking so loudly?

She glanced over at Julia Butler, who was staring at her husband. But Mrs. Butler didn't look puzzled. She looked worried.

"Julia, dear, why don't you walk Molly to the drive," Mr. Butler said. He smiled down at Molly and held out his hand to her. He shook her hand, adding, "Thank you for coming to visit, Molly. I'm sorry I couldn't spend more time with you and Mrs. Butler."

"But I don't understand," Molly said. "Sultan . . ."

"Yes, I'll be sure to bring Sultan by the forge tomorrow morning," Mr. Butler interrupted in the same loud voice. "Now, my dear, you'd better be on your way."

With that, he turned and stepped back through the doorway into the room filled with British officers.

Molly and Mrs. Butler left the porch and walked through the garden to the drive in front of the house. Thomas Cole was waiting there with the strawberry roan and Flora. He helped Molly into the saddle, then mounted his own horse.

"Thank you for inviting me, Mrs. Butler," Molly said. "I had a wonderful time."

The worried expression left Mrs. Butler's face and she smiled warmly at Molly. "I'm glad," she said. "And I hope you'll come to see us again very soon."

As she and Thomas rode along, Molly thought about Mr. Butler's strange behavior and Mrs. Butler's worried look. She was sure that the clue to why they had acted the way they did was in the note tucked inside her pocket. She had to find out what was written in the note. But she didn't want to read the note in front of Thomas. How could she get rid of him for a while?

Molly shook her head with frustration. It was then that she discovered she wasn't wearing her straw hat. That gave her an idea. She brought Flora to a halt. At the same time, Thomas stopped the strawberry roan.

"What's wrong?" Thomas asked. "Why did you stop?"

"I just remembered that I left my hat on the porch at Brookfield Farm," Molly told him. "Ma will be upset if I come home without it." She gave him her best smile. "Would you mind going back and getting it for me? Please?"

Thomas nodded, turned his horse around, and cantered off in the direction of Brookfield Farm.

Molly waited until he was out of sight. Then she slid off Flora and led the mare to an oak tree. She sat on a grassy hump under the tree, reached into her pocket, pulled out the paper, and unfolded it. When

she saw what was written on it, she blinked in surprise.

"It's just letters, numbers, and dates with question marks written after them," she murmured. "None of it makes any sense." Disappointed, she folded up the paper and put it back in her pocket.

Soon, Thomas came cantering up to her. "Here's your hat," he said breathlessly.

"Thank you, Thomas," Molly said as she tied the straw hat on her head.

When they reached the Randalls' home, Molly stopped in front of the forge. She thanked Thomas for taking her to Brookfield Farm and back. Then she quickly dismounted, tied Flora to a post outside the forge, and ran into the building. Her father was there alone, using the bellows to stoke up the forge fire.

She held out the note. "Mr. Butler asked me to give you this."

Her father took the note and unfolded it. Molly waited while he studied the note for several minutes. She hoped he would tell her why Mr. Butler had written it and what it meant. But he didn't. Instead he refolded the paper and said calmly, "I think you'd better let your mother know you're home."

"Yes, Pa," Molly said. She slowly walked across the room to the doorway.

"Close the door on your way out, will you?" she heard Pa call out.

Molly turned to shut the door. As she did, she saw her father drop the note from Richard Butler into the forge fire.

Molly gently shut the door behind her. Now she was sure that Mr. Butler had written something very important in that note. And she was determined to find out what it was!

The Mystery in
the Barn

That night, Molly had a dream. In it, she was walking through a large stable past dozens of beautiful Arabian horses. When she came to Sultan's stall, she asked a stable hand to saddle him up. Then she and Sultan galloped off across empty fields in the moonlight. Suddenly, a bright light flashed in their eyes. Sultan let out a loud whinny and reared up in fright.

Molly woke up with a start. One of the horses is whinnying, she thought. Or am I still dreaming? She lay still and listened. A moment later, she heard it again. Molly was sure it was Flora who had whinnied. Was something wrong with her?

Molly threw back the quilt and got out of bed. She tiptoed across the dark room to the peg on the wall to get her dress. As she did, she stepped on a squeaky floor board. She froze, hoping the sound hadn't awakened her sister. Anne muttered something in her sleep and rolled over. Then the room was silent once more. Molly dressed as quietly and as quickly as she could. She picked up her shoes and padded out of the room to the front door. She slipped out of the house, closing the door softly behind her, and sat on the front step to put on her shoes.

The night was warm and muggy, and there was a full moon covered with clouds. The barn and the forge were ghostly shapes in the weak moonlight. As Molly was rounding the house, she suddenly saw a light flashing from the window on the right side of the barn. A few moments later, two men came walking up the meadow toward the barn carrying something between them. Molly could barely make out the shape of a large box. She hid behind a dogwood tree near the house and watched as the men passed the box through the window to someone inside the barn. One of the men ran back down the meadow. The other man climbed through the window into the barn.

Molly crept out from behind the tree and ran over to the hayloft on the left side of the barn. She stepped onto the ladder that led to the hayloft and climbed up. When she reached the top, she stepped over the last rung into the hayloft and crouched down in the hay.

The first voice she heard was her father's.

"How many muskets are in the shipment?" John Randall was asking.

"Six dozen," replied the other man. "That makes a total of one-hundred-and-forty-four muskets you've hidden.

Molly knew that voice. She hadn't heard it for several years, but she still recognized it. She crept through the hay on her hands and knees until she was able to peek over the edge. She saw her father standing in front of Flora's empty stall, holding up a brightly lit lantern. Facing him was Molly's uncle, William Randall. He was shorter and stockier than his older brother, and his hair was a darker brown. He was dressed in a fringed buckskin shirt and buckskin pants. Molly's uncle was a major in the American army, but he was supposed to be serving with General George Washington in New York. What was he doing here?

Molly looked around for Flora and saw her standing on a bed of straw at the far end of the barn, away from the other horses. Then she noticed something else. All the straw had been cleared out of

Flora's stall, and the floor was completely bare. The floorboards had been pried up, leaving a large hollow space. Kneeling in front of the hollowed-out area was her brother.

Ethan looked over at his father and uncle and asked, "Is this space large enough for one more box of muskets?"

"It should be," his father replied. "It's the same space we hollowed out in the stall Sweetbriar is using."

"You're too softhearted, John, when it comes to horses," Uncle William said. "I'm not sure I would have risked discovery of our smuggling operation just to care for a couple of redcoats' horses!" He shook his head slowly at his brother, but there was an affectionate smile on his face.

"Come now, Will," Pa said, "it would have looked suspicious if I had refused to take their horses."

Molly inched forward, hoping to hear and see more.

"Ethan, why don't you go down to the boat and see if Private Kempton is ready to bring up the third box," her uncle said.

"I will," Ethan said, getting to his feet. "But I don't see why we have to go in and out of the window. It's safe to use the double doors at this time of night.

There's no one around."

"It's better to be cautious," Pa warned him. "I heard in town yesterday that there have been British patrols on the main road late at night."

After Ethan had left the barn, Uncle William turned to his brother and said, "I know you think Ethan's too young to be a soldier. But I'm glad you gave in and let him join my regiment. We can use able young men like him."

"Caroline and I are not happy about it, Will," Molly's father admitted. "But the lad was getting restless. He felt he wasn't doing enough for the patriot cause. I only wish I could do more."

"You're doing plenty right here," William insisted heartily, clapping his brother on the back.

Up in the hayloft, Molly's heart beat with excitement. Ethan was going to be an American soldier! She felt very proud of him. But at the same time, she was scared for him. What if he had to fight in a battle?

Just then, she heard her father mention Richard Butler, and she crept forward in the hay just a little bit further.

"The note was very detailed," Pa was saying. "Butler has a real talent for getting information out of British officers. His note gave us the exact number of

Cornwallis's troops here in Yorktown and where they would be positioned during a battle. It also suggested several dates for the arrival of fresh troops from General Henry Clinton in New York, and the number of soldiers that are expected." He ran down the list of numbers and dates Molly remembered reading in Richard Butler's note.

By now she was so excited, it was hard for her to keep still. From the way her father was talking, it sounded as if Mr. Butler was a spy for the Americans and not a Tory at all!

"By the time General Clinton decides to send troops to Yorktown, if he does, General Washington and his men will be here," William said with a grin. "These muskets will come in handy for the town's defense. By the way, is Butler sure Cornwallis knows nothing yet of Washington's advance upon Yorktown?"

John Randall nodded. "Completely sure. It's not been easy for him to pretend to be a Tory, when all the time he's been on our side."

At that moment, Ethan tapped on the window shutter. John Randall hung the lantern on a hook, and went over to the window. He threw open the shutters, and with Uncle William's help, lifted a box of muskets into the barn.

Molly wanted a clearer view, so she crawled even

closer to the edge of the hayloft. Suddenly, she felt herself begin to fall. "Help!" she yelled, as she hit the soft haystack below her in a shower of hay. Molly's shout startled the horses, who began to whinny and dance nervously. Ethan hurried to calm them down.

"Molly!" exclaimed her father, dropping his end of the box and rushing over to her. "Are you hurt?"

"N-No, I don't think so," she stammered, as she struggled to sit up.

Pa helped her to her feet. "How long have you been hiding up there, young lady?" he asked her sternly. "And how much did you hear?"

Molly told him how she had crept out of the house after hearing Flora whinny, and what she had seen and heard. When she finished, Uncle William began to chuckle.

"You'd make a good spy, Molly," he said, his eyes twinkling. "I can't believe you were hiding in the hayloft all this time, and we never even suspected it! Until you fell into the haystack, that is."

"She has to learn that this isn't a game, Will," Molly's father said sharply. He looked at his daughter with a serious expression. "We're all in danger Molly. No one must ever know about our smuggling muskets, or that Richard Butler is an American spy. Do you understand that?"

"Yes, Pa," Molly said soberly. "I understand. I won't let you down, I promise."

"Good," Pa said briskly. "Now, I want you to go back to the house with Ethan. You can help him pack and get some food to take with him."

Molly nodded and started for the door. "I think you'd better use the window, like the rest of us," Uncle William said, with a grin. "Unless you'd rather go out the way you came in—through the hayloft."

"I think I've had enough of that hayloft for one night," Molly replied, smiling back at him.

Ethan climbed through the window first, then helped Molly outside. The air had cooled off, and Molly shivered a little. "How does Uncle William smuggle muskets to us?" she asked her brother as they walked toward the house. "And where are the rest of his soldiers?"

"He uses a small ship disguised as a British gunboat," Ethan explained. "And his men have camped in a hideout about twenty miles upriver. Uncle William and his men were sent to Virginia by General Washington to get information on Cornwallis's troops, and to pave the way for an American invasion. It was very exciting when Pa told us about it."

"Us? What do you mean us?" Molly demanded, stopping short.

Ethan looked uncomfortable. "Um, I mean me, Anne, and Ma."

"You mean everyone knew about Uncle William and the smuggling except me?" Molly said in a shrill voice.

"Keep your voice down," Ethan said sharply. Then he gently took his sister by the shoulders. "It was for your own safety, Molly. Ma and Pa thought it would be better if you didn't know. But I think that was a mistake. If we had told you, maybe you wouldn't have sneaked into the barn and scared all the horses."

"Well, I didn't want to fall out of the hayloft, Ethan," Molly retorted. But she felt better than she had a few moments earlier. At least Ethan was beginning to realize that she was grown-up enough to share family secrets.

As soon as she stepped into the house, Molly saw her mother and Anne. They were sitting by the stove in the main room, fully dressed.

"We got up to say good-bye to Ethan," Anne said, jumping up from the rocking chair and rushing over to them. "Then we heard Molly shouting and the horses whinnying. What happened?"

Molly and Ethan took turns telling them. Molly's mother shook her head. "What am I going to do with you, Molly Randall," she said with a sigh. Then she stood up. "Well, what's done is done. Anne, come with me to the kitchen, and we'll prepare a food basket for your brother."

Ethan headed up to his loft to pack up a few pieces of clothing. Molly was left standing in the middle of the room without anything to do. Then she had an idea. She ran into her room and began searching through the cupboard. Soon she found what she was looking for. It was a little silver horseshoe made by her grandfather, a silversmith.

Grasping the horseshoe, Molly ran back to the main room. Ethan was just climbing down from the loft, a cloth bundle slung over his shoulder.

"Here, Ethan," Molly said, holding out the horseshoe. "I want you to have this."

Ethan shook his head. "I can't take it, Molly. Grandfather Burke gave you that horseshoe for your tenth birthday. I know how much you love it."

Molly took his hand, put the little silver horseshoe in it, and closed up the fingers. "It's for good luck," she said. "And to help you remember how much we all love you. Please take it."

"All right," Ethan said, smiling warmly at his sister. He put his arm around her and hugged her tightly.

Just then, Molly's mother and sister came into the room carrying a large basket. Ethan hugged them both, then picked up the basket. Molly held the door open for him.

"Don't worry about me, ladies," he said with a grin. "I'll be fine." Then he turned, stepped out the door, and was gone.

"All right, girls," Ma said, her voice trembling. "Back to bed." Molly and Anne silently obeyed.

It took Molly a long time to get to sleep. She kept thinking of all the exciting things that had happened. And she had a feeling that the excitement wasn't over. The Randalls weren't sitting on the sidelines of the American Revolution any longer. Now they were part of the war, too!

CHAPTER SIX

Molly's New Job

Molly was the first one up the next morning. She wanted to talk to both of her parents in private, without Anne being there. She had something very important to ask them. And she was sure Anne would make a fuss if she knew what it was.

She got out of bed and dressed. Then, tiptoeing past her sleeping sister, she left the room. She could hear Ma and Pa moving around in their bedroom and talking in low tones to each other. She went out to the kitchen and sat down at the table to wait for them.

Several minutes later, Ma and Pa walked into the room. They both looked surprised to find Molly there.

"What are you doing up so early?" her mother

asked as she took the kettle off the shelf over the fireplace. She looked at her daughter anxiously, then stepped over to her and felt her forehead. "Are you feeling well?"

"I feel fine, Ma," Molly said. "It's just that I need to talk to you and Pa about something.

"What's so important that you had to get up at the crack of dawn to ask us?" her father asked smiling.

"Well," Molly began, "now that Ethan is gone, you'll need someone to help you in the forge."

"Yes," Pa said, nodding. "I had thought of asking Richard Butler if Thomas Cole could be spared to work for me. The lad wants to be a blacksmith and has a real way with horses."

Molly's face fell. It hadn't occurred to her that her father would think of Thomas Cole to take Ethan's place in the forge. But then she suddenly remembered something Thomas had said to her yesterday.

"I don't think Thomas will be able to work here," she said to her father. "Mr. Butler has two lame horses, and Thomas is responsible for them. Thomas told me so himself, when we were riding back from Brookfield Farm."

She took a deep breath and went on. "So, I was hoping that you would let me work in the forge. Will you, Pa?"

Her father was silent for a moment. Then Pa shook his head slowly. "I don't know, Molly, It's very, very . . ."

"Dangerous, I understand that," Molly finished. "But I promise to be careful. Please let me do it, Pa."

"What do you think, Caroline?" Pa asked his wife. "Can you do without Molly in the house for awhile?"

"I think we'll manage," Ma said. "But I don't want you hammering horseshoes or pulling them from the fire, Molly. You can hold the horses and fetch tools for your father. And it's still your responsibility to care for Flora and the other two horses. Is that understood?"

"Oh, yes, Ma," Molly said, her eyes shining. She jumped up and hugged first her mother and then her father. "I'll do a good job, Pa, you'll see."

"I'm sure you will, daughter," Pa said with a laugh. "Now, let's get something to drink before we get started."

"Get started doing what?" Anne's sleepy voice asked from the doorway.

Molly hesitated a moment before answering her sister. She knew Anne wasn't going to be happy at the news. "Um, Ma and Pa are letting me work in the forge," she said finally.

"But that means I'll have to do Molly's chores as well as my own," Anne said crossly. "She's just doing this because she hates working in the house."

Molly had to admit to herself that her sister was right. She didn't like the kinds of tasks her mother and Anne worked at, like cooking, cleaning, washing, and sewing. She would much rather be with the horses and with Pa in the forge. But she also knew she wasn't just trying to get out of doing her regular chores. Pa needed her help.

"I understand why you feel it's not fair," Ma said, putting her arm around Anne. "But it makes sense for Molly to help your father. Meanwhile, the two of us will just have to do the best we can."

"At least you won't have to keep reminding me to do my chores," Molly said with a grin. "I know you hate that."

"Speaking of reminders," Pa said, putting down his mug. "It's time to get to work."

"I'm on my way," Molly told him, getting up from the table.

She ran out to the barn and pulled open one of the double doors. Inside, everything was back to normal. Daisy and the horses were standing peacefully in their stalls in the straw. It was as if the smuggling operation of last night had never happened.

Molly fed and watered the three horses. She was pleased to see that Pepper and Sweetbriar were looking bright-eyed and seemed to be a bit fatter than they had been two days ago.

After she had turned the horses out into the meadow and cleaned out their stalls, Molly joined her father in the forge. The first customer of the day arrived at the same time. It was Thomas Cole's father, Daniel. Mr. Cole had brought his sorrel gelding, Red, to be shod.

"Where's Ethan?" Mr. Cole asked, as Molly led Red into the forge. "Why isn't he working with you, John?"

Molly looked questioningly at her father. How were they going to explain to customers why Ethan wasn't at the forge? Without hesitating, he said, "I felt that Ethan needed a change, Daniel. He had been talking about joining the colonial army, but Caroline and I felt he was too young. So, I sent him to live with Caroline's brother and sister-in-law for awhile. They own a farm up-country."

Mr. Cole looked at Molly and knit his brows. "Well, I hope your daughter knows what she's doing with my Red. Perhaps I'd better hold onto him. He can be skittish."

"I know what to do, Mr. Cole," Molly insisted, grasping Red's halter firmly. "Please don't worry."

She stroked the sorrel's neck and talked to him quietly while her father removed the old shoes and trimmed his hoofs. Then Pa took the red-hot shoes out of the forge fire with his tongs. After hammering the shoe into shape on the anvil, he carried it over to Red. He placed the hot shoe on Red's front hoof, where it began to sizzle and smoke. Red's eyes rolled back in his head. He snorted nervously and tried to toss his head, but Molly kept a firm hold on his halter. She knew that Red wasn't in pain from the red-hot shoe because the bottom of his hoof had no feeling. The smell of smoke and the sizzling sound had just made him anxious.

"It's all right, boy," she said gently several times, and finally the gelding became calmer.

Pa plunged the hot shoe into a bucket of cold water. When it was cool enough to handle, he began to nail it on, first with several short, light taps, and then with two hard blows to push the nail through the outside of the hoof wall. After all the nails were in place, Pa straightened up. "Good job, Molly," he said with an encouraging smile. "Three more shoes to go. Keep holding on to him, just as you're doing."

Molly grinned proudly. She hoped Mr. Cole had heard her father praise her. She looked over at the open doorway where he had been standing and saw Captain Foster and Lieutenant Hayden just stepping into the forge.

"Yes, gentlemen?" John Randall said, looking up from the forge fire. "What is it you want?"

"We are looking for our horses," Lieutenant Hayden told him. "They aren't in the barn. Can you tell us where to find them?"

"I believe they're in the meadow, behind the house," Pa said. "Is that right, Molly?"

Molly didn't answer for a moment. She was afraid the redcoats were ready to take Pepper and Sweetbriar away. Finally she answered. "Yes, they're in the meadow. But they're still thin and weak."

Captain Foster smiled at her. "We know that, young lady. We just want to see how they are."

Meanwhile, Lieutenant Hayden had been glancing around the forge. "Where's your hothead of a son, Randall?" he asked suddenly. "I understood it was he who worked with you, not your daughter."

Molly's stomach turned over in fear. Would the redcoats believe her father's lie about Ethan as easily as Daniel Cole had?

She held her breath while her father repeated the story he had told to Daniel Cole. Both officers seemed satisfied with his explanation, and Molly breathed a deep sigh of relief.

After the officers had left, Molly said in a low voice, "Do you think they asked you about Ethan because they suspect something, Pa?"

"I don't know, Molly," Pa said honestly. "We'll hope not. Now, let's get the rest of these shoes on Red. Other customers will be coming soon."

By late afternoon Molly had helped her father shoe six horses. After the last horse had been sent home with his owner, Molly's mother came into the forge, carrying a basket.

"I was hoping you could spare Molly for a little while," she said to her husband. "I would like her to take a chicken pie and some preserves to Aunt Abigail. With all the excitement, I feel we have been neglecting her lately."

Abigail Burke was Caroline Randall's elderly great-aunt. She was a proud, stubborn woman who never set foot outside her home except to attend weddings, christenings, and funerals. Molly dreaded visits to Aunt Abigail. She hoped her father would say that he was too busy to let her go.

Instead, he said, "That will be fine, Caroline. I don't think there will be many customers coming in now."

"Why can't Anne go?" Molly asked her mother.

"Anne is lying down with a headache," Ma said, giving Molly her "no-nonsense" look.

Sighing, Molly took the basket from her mother

and left the forge. "Mr. Butler and Sultan will probably come by while I'm gone," she muttered as she trudged down the road toward the town. "It's not fair!"

After Molly had passed three cottages, she came to Aunt Abigail's. It was a small brick house with a polished oak door and a brass door knocker. Molly stepped up to the door, lifted the door knocker, and let it fall.

A few moments later, the door opened, and Aunt Abigail stood before her. As usual, she was dressed in black, with a white mobcap covering her silvery gray hair. She was tall and thin, with piercing blue eyes.

"Well, come in, girl," Aunt Abigail said crossly. "What are you waiting for?"

"Um, nothing, ma'am," Molly mumbled, stepping into the house. She followed Aunt Abigail to the parlor and sat down on a straight-backed chair near the window that faced the road.

"Did you leave your manners at home, miss?" snapped her aunt.

Molly immediately jumped up from her chair. She waited for the older woman to sit down. Then she sat down again with the basket on her knees. The chair was hard and uncomfortable, and Molly squirmed.

"How is your mother?" Aunt Abigail asked crisply. "Why didn't she come to visit me? Speak up, girl. And please do stop all that fidgeting!"

Molly stopped squirming and sat still. "Um, she's been very busy, ma'am," she replied. "But she sent me to bring you a chicken pie and some peach preserves."

Aunt Abigail raised her head slightly and peered over at the basket. "Hmm, that was thoughtful of her. But then, your mother always was thoughtful. Your grandmother and I saw to it that the Burke girls were taught good manners. I well remember when . . ."

Oh, no, thought Molly, not another story about the Burkes and their good manners. She tried to keep still and listen, but the more she tried, the harder the chair felt. She began to peek through the window out of the corner of her eye. Suddenly, she saw a man hurry by the window. It was Richard Butler. Where was he going? And where was Sultan?

Molly was sure that something was wrong. She stood up quickly, knocking the basket to the floor. "I'm sorry, Aunt Abigail, but I must go at once. Please excuse me!"

"Well, of all the rude young . . ." were the last words she heard as she rushed out of her aunt's house.

"Mr. Butler!" she called, running up the road toward him.

Richard Butler stopped and turned around. When

Molly caught up to him, he put his hands on her shoulders, looked into her eyes, and said urgently, "Listen to me, Molly, for there's very little time. The British have discovered that I'm an American spy and plan to arrest me at any moment. It's certain that they'll take my horses as well. I managed to send word to Julia to escape. But there's Sultan. He's waiting for me over at Mr. Gresham's. I didn't have time to get him. Will you save him?"

Molly nodded. "Of course I will. Don't worry, Mr. Butler. The redcoats will never get Sultan."

"You there, Butler!" a voice suddenly barked from behind Molly. She turned and saw six armed redcoats marching toward them, led by an officer. "Surrender, Butler!" commanded the officer. "Surrender peacefully or we'll shoot!"

He and his men raised their muskets and aimed them at Richard Butler.

CHAPTER SEVEN

Scary News

Molly felt an arm around her shoulders. "Goodbye, Molly," Richard Butler said quietly. "With luck we'll meet again." He hugged her quickly and stepped up to the officer with his arms raised. "I surrender," he said calmly.

The officer motioned to two of his men. The men grabbed Richard Butler's arms and swiftly tied them behind his back. The officer looked over at Molly and said gruffly, "You, girl! You're free to go."

Molly gulped and nodded. She started to walk up the road, but her legs felt shaky, and she had to stop. She turned and saw Mr. Butler surrounded by soldiers being led into town. They stopped at a brick building next to the large house General Cornwallis used as his headquarters. Molly knew that the building where they had taken Mr. Butler was the town jail.

Molly watched until the soldiers and Mr. Butler had disappeared into the building. Then she walked back toward Aunt Abigail's house. She was relieved to find that her legs had stopped shaking. She passed her aunt's house quickly, afraid that at any moment Aunt Abigail would yank open the door and demand to know why she had run off.

She passed several more small houses until she came to a lane that led down to the river. At the end of the lane was the large house belonging to Francis Gresham.

Molly hurried down the lane. When she reached the house, she looked around quickly. There was a path by the house that led around to the stable. Molly sneaked down the path, hardly daring to breathe for fear of being discovered. At the back of the house was a garden with a tall hedge at one end. There was an opening in the middle of the hedge. Through the opening, Molly could see the stable. She continued down the path to where the hedge stopped. As she rounded the hedge and made her way to the stable, she suddenly saw two young men step out of the building and walk toward her. She recognized them.

They were Ethan's age, and they worked for Mr. Gresham as stable hands. One of them was Sam Thomas, the son of Josiah Thomas, the ironmonger.

She desperately looked around for somewhere to hide and saw a clump of bushes a few feet away. She crouched down behind it. The voices of the two boys became louder, and soon she was able to hear what they were saying.

"The redcoats can question my father and me all they want," Sam Thomas said smugly. "We have nothing to hide. Not like the Randalls."

"What do you mean?" asked the other boy.

"My father was talking to a redcoat lieutenant today," Sam replied. "His name was Hayden. Well, Hayden thinks it's very suspicious that Ethan Randall has left town so suddenly. He suspects that Ethan might have been working with Richard Butler as a spy."

The voices of the two boys grew fainter as they moved past Molly. But she had heard enough. Now she knew that for sure Lieutenant Hayden hadn't believed her father's lie about Ethan. She was glad that her brother was safe with Uncle William, but she also knew that her brother and uncle would have to be warned to be extra careful during their smuggling runs.

Molly peeked out from behind the bushes and saw that the boys had gone. She straightened up and ran over to the stable as fast as she could. She pushed open the door, stepped inside, and softly called out, "Sultan."

From a stall on the left came an answering nicker. Molly hurried over to the stall and saw the Arabian standing patiently. He turned his head to look at Molly as she entered the stall.

"You're coming home with me, boy," Molly told him, trying to sound as calm as possible. She stroked his neck gently as she glanced around the stall for his lead rope. She found it and slipped it onto Sultan's halter. Then she took hold of the halter strap under Sultan's chin and took a deep breath.

"All right, boy, back up now," Molly told the Arabian as she stepped forward. Sultan snorted and tried to toss his head, but Molly kept a firm hold on his halter. She continued to talk to him in encouraging tones, while moving forward, and eventually the Arabian began to back out of the stall.

When he was all the way out, Molly grasped the lead rope and gently tugged on it. "Come on, Sultan," she urged. "Come on, boy." After a moment, Sultan moved forward.

Molly led Sultan out of the stable, but instead of

walking him back down the path, she went toward the other side of the hedge. That way, beyond the hedge, lay the fields and marshland that ran alongside the river. Molly knew that by walking across the fields, they could avoid people. She didn't want them to run into any redcoats on the way home.

When they reached the Randalls' house, Molly saw that the meadow was empty. She opened the gate, unclipped Sultan's lead rope, and stepped away from the Arabian. Sultan tossed his head and lifted his tail. Then he cantered into the meadow and with a loud neigh reared up on his hind legs. Molly gazed with wonder at the sight of the beautiful gray Arabian silhouetted against the dark blue sky.

When she stepped into the house several moments later, she found her family in the kitchen eating supper.

"I'm glad you're back, Molly," Ma said, getting up to fetch a plate and a mug for her. "I was beginning to worry."

"Were you having such a good time at Aunt Abigail's that you didn't want to leave?" Anne asked in a teasing tone.

"Not exactly," Molly answered. She told them what had happened to Richard Butler, the boys' conversation about Ethan, and how she had brought

Sultan home with her.

"I'm glad you could bring Sultan here," Pa said when Molly had finished telling her story. "But that is very bad news about Butler. We'll just have to hope that the redcoats don't make him reveal our smuggling operation."

"There is one thing you can be sure of, John," Ma pointed out. "Lieutenant Hayden and Captain Foster will be coming here more often, now that they're suspicious of Ethan."

Molly's father nodded in agreement. "That means we all have to watch very carefully what we say and do. Right, girls?"

"Yes, Pa," Molly and Anne said in unison.

After supper, Pa left the house to bring Sultan in to the one empty stall in the barn. Molly wanted to do it, but Ma insisted that she stay inside and rest. Then she handed her younger daughter a sock, a darning needle, and some thread.

But as Molly darned away at the sock, she couldn't help but think of Richard Butler. Maybe it's my fault he was arrested, she thought. If I hadn't run after him, he might have gotten away. But if he had escaped from the redcoats, what would have happened to Sultan?

In bed later that evening, Molly was so worried

about Mr. Butler that she could not fall asleep. Finally she turned toward her sister. "Anne," she said in a loud whisper. "Anne!"

"Hmm?" Anne said sleepily. She opened her eyes. "What is it, Molly?"

"What do you think the redcoats will do to Mr. Butler?" Molly asked.

"Do?" her sister replied with a yawn. "Well, he's a spy, isn't he? They'll hang him, of course."

"Hang him!" Molly cried, sitting up in bed. "That's not true. You're making it up!"

"Oh, grow up, Molly," Anne said crossly. She turned over and went back to sleep.

Molly stared at her sister for a moment. Then she jumped out of bed and rushed out of the room. She ran out of the house and down to the barn. She pulled open the door and went straight to Sultan's stall.

Molly threw her arms around Sultan and buried her face in his mane. "It's my fault," she cried. "Mr. Butler's going to be hanged because of me. If I could just stop the redcoats from hanging him. But what can I do?"

Sultan turned his head and nuzzled Molly's arm. Suddenly, she heard someone calling out her name in a low voice. She lifted her head and saw her Uncle William entering the barn. Behind him was her

mother. Both of them looked very worried.

Molly hastily brushed the tears from her eyes and hurried over to them. "What's happened?" she asked anxiously. "Why are you here, Ma?"

"It's Ethan," Uncle William explained. "And I'm afraid it's bad news. When he was unloading a box of muskets a little while ago, he slipped and fell. He may have broken his leg."

"Pa and Private Kempton are bringing him up to the barn now," said her mother.

At that moment, Molly saw her father enter the barn carrying her brother by the shoulders. Private Kempton was holding Ethan's legs. On one of the legs was a wooden splint. Ethan was moaning softly with pain. They laid him gently down on the same pile of hay Molly had fallen into the night before. Molly's mother rushed over and knelt beside him.

"Is there anything I can do, Pa?" Molly asked.

Pa nodded. "Yes, Molly, there is. I want you and Anne to go to the village, fetch Dr. Ellison, and bring him here."

"Can Ellison be trusted, John?" Uncle William asked with a frown.

"I'm sure of it," Molly's father replied. "He's even spent some time in prison for speaking out against British rule. He's a true patriot." He turned to Molly and said urgently. "You must go now, daughter. There's no time to waste."

Molly ran out of the barn and back to the house. She hurried to her room, leaned over Anne's bed, and began to shake her sister by the shoulder. "Wake up, Anne," she cried. "Wake up!"

Her sister opened her eyes. "What is it now, Molly?" she asked in a grumpy tone.

"Ethan's broken his leg, and we have to fetch Dr. Ellison," Molly told her in a rush. She grabbed her clothes and began to dress quickly. Then she hurried out to the kitchen and took the lantern off the hook by the door. She took the candle out of the lantern and lit it from the burning embers in the fireplace. Then she placed the candle back in the lantern and shut the little glass door.

When she returned to the main room, Anne was dressed and waiting by the door. The sisters left the house and started down the dark road. Molly held the lantern in front of them so that they could see the path before them. The lantern cast eerie shadows all around them, and the only sounds came from the crickets in the underbrush.

"Dr. Ellison's house is just a few houses past Cornwallis's headquarters," Anne said after they had been walking for awhile at a fast pace. "We're nearly at Cornwallis's house now."

As they approached the British general's house, Molly suddenly saw a line of redcoats loom up at them out of the darkness. She grabbed her sister's hand. "Keep going," she whispered. "We have to get the doctor."

But before they could pass the house, one of the redcoats stepped up to them and held up his hand. "Halt!" he ordered sternly. "No one is allowed to go any further!"

Dodging Redcoats

"What do we do now?" Anne whispered.

Molly thought fast. She looked up at the redcoat, her eyes wide with distress. "Oh, please, sir," she said in a pleading tone. "Our mother has a fever and Pa has sent my sister and me to fetch the doctor. Please let us pass."

"What's going on here, Corporal?" another redcoat asked, breaking through the line and stepping up to them. With a start, Molly recognized Captain Foster.

"This girl says her ma's sick," the corporal told him. "She wants to get Dr. Ellison."

"Let them through," Captain Foster said quietly. "I know these girls. They're the blacksmith's daughters."

"But, sir, I have my orders to enforce the curfew," protested the corporal. "No one is allowed out on the street after 11:00 P.M."

"I know quite well what the curfew is, Corporal," snapped the captain. "And I am telling you to let these children fetch the doctor."

The corporal stood at attention and saluted. "Yes, sir," he said. He motioned to his men to stand aside so that Molly and Anne could pass.

"Th-thank you, sir," Molly stammered to the captain.

"You don't have to thank me, Molly," Captain Foster said. "But be quick. I'm going off duty soon, and my replacement is a stickler about curfew."

Molly and Anne didn't have to be told twice. They hurried past Cornwallis's house, and several seconds later came to Dr. James Ellison's house.

Dr. Ellison answered Anne's knock. He was holding a book in his hand and was still dressed. He was a balding, heavyset man in his late forties. He ushered Molly and Anne into the house and listened carefully as they told him what had happened to Ethan. Then, without a word, he grabbed his hat and medical bag, and led the way out of the house.

None of them spoke until they were well past the line of soldiers in front of Cornwallis's house. Then Dr.

Ellison asked, "How did you girls manage to get past the redcoats?"

"Captain Foster let us through," Anne explained. "He and Lieutenant Hayden are stabling their horses in our barn. Maybe he thought he owed us a favor."

"It's possible," the doctor said. "Foster is a good man, I'll admit. But he's still a redcoat."

When they reached the Randalls' barn, Molly noticed that Uncle William and Private Kempton were gone. Ethan was still lying on the pile of hay.

"Thank you for coming, Jim," Pa said hurrying over to greet the doctor.

Dr. Ellison nodded and knelt beside Ethan. After examining Molly's brother for several minutes, he looked up and said, "Well, his leg's broken all right. But whoever made this splint did a good job. I won't have to reset the leg." He saw that Pa was about to speak, and he held up his hand. "Don't tell me who set the leg, John. It's better if I don't know." He stood up. "I'll give you a recipe for a hot herbal drink that will dull the pain and keep him from getting a fever. And he shouldn't be moved."

"But he can't stay here," Ma told him anxiously. "Lieutenant Hayden suspects him of spying with Richard Butler. He must be hidden."

"Not in the house," Pa said. "That would be the

first place they'd look."

"What about the hayloft?" Molly suggested, thinking of how she had managed to hide there.

"They might want to search the hayloft, too," Pa pointed out. "But I agree. It's the best solution for now. Will you help me with Ethan, Jim?"

Slowly and carefully, Pa and Dr. Ellison lifted Ethan from the pile of hay and carried him up the ladder to the hayloft. When they had settled him in the hay and climbed down, Ma lifted her skirts and started up the ladder.

"What are you doing, Ma?" asked Molly.

"I'm going to stay here with Ethan, at least for tonight," her mother replied. "I want you girls to prepare the herbal drink Dr. Ellison suggested and bring it to me. And we'll need pillows and blankets, too."

Ethan struggled to raise himself up on his elbows. "You don't have to stay here, Ma," he whispered wearily.

"I'm staying, and that's final," his mother said firmly as she gently pushed him back in the hay.

Dr. Ellison told Molly and Anne how to mix the herbal drink, then he picked up his hat and bag. "I'll look in on Ethan tomorrow."

He took the lantern that Molly's father held out to

him and then he left the house.

The next few days were busy ones. Molly helped Pa in the forge, took care of Sultan and the other horses, and helped look after Ethan. When she had a free moment, she ran out to the meadow to watch Sultan. The powerful Arabian and gentle Flora had become good friends, grazing together and sometimes nuzzling each other. Pepper and Sweetbriar were spending less and less time in the meadow. They had grown much healthier and more high-spirited, and Captain Foster and Lieutenant Hayden came by every afternoon to take them out for exercise. When Molly saw them coming, she would hurry to the barn to warn Ethan. Then Ethan would lie still, and Molly would busy herself with chores in the barn until the officers had saddled up their horses and left.

Captain Foster and Lieutenant Hayden never asked any of the Randalls about Ethan. Molly was relieved, but she was also surprised. When she asked her father about it, he said, "They may feel that a seventeen-year-old boy isn't worth worrying about, now that they've captured Richard Butler."

Pa's mentioning of Mr. Butler made Molly feel a prick of fear. For two days now they hadn't heard any more news about him. Had he been hanged?

Early that morning, Molly was leading Marigold into the forge so that her father could replace a shoe the mare had lost. As usual, Josiah Thomas chatted away while her father worked. Marigold was skittish, and Molly had to concentrate hard on keeping her still and soothing her down. At first she wasn't paying much attention to what the ironmonger was saying. Then he started to talk about Richard Butler, and she began to listen.

"And to think he fooled us all into thinking he was a Tory," she heard him say with a laugh. "I'd have thought that they would have hanged him by now, but he's still sitting in jail. From what I hear, Cornwallis hasn't even questioned him yet. The general is too busy strengthening his troops in Yorktown and sending messages to General Clinton in New York to ask for more troops."

Molly felt a wave of relief wash over her. Mr. Butler was still alive! But for how long, she wondered.

After Molly's father was finished with Marigold and Josiah Thomas had led her away, Molly went over to the barn to see to the horses. She decided to save Sultan for last, so that she could spend more time with him. She groomed him slowly and carefully, combing his mane and brushing the tangles out of his tail gently, a few hairs at a time. By now, Sultan was used to her touch, and he stood patiently while she worked on him. When she began to back him out of his stall, he didn't balk, but moved backward obediently.

"Sultan looks really beautiful, Molly," she heard Ethan say. "You've done a good job taking care of him."

Molly glanced up at her brother, who was sitting in the hayloft with his back against the barn wall. "Thank you," she said, grinning at Sultan proudly. Then she untied his lead rope and led him out to the meadow.

After the afternoon meal, Molly went with her father to shoe a horse that belonged to a farmer who lived a few miles outside of Yorktown. She rode Flora, and her father rode Sultan. Molly was careful to watch how her father handled the Arabian. She noticed that Pa was firm but gentle with Sultan, and always let him know that he was in control. She watched his stance closely as he mounted Sultan and as he pulled on the reins to guide him.

Molly and her father arrived back home in the late afternoon. "I'll unsaddle the horses and rub them down," Molly offered as they rode into the barn. "I saw a customer waiting for you at the forge. It's a redcoat."

John Randall nodded. "Yes, I know. He came by

yesterday while you were bringing the horses in to ask me if I would shoe his horse. The army blacksmith is too busy to do it."

Molly dismounted, unsaddled Flora, and removed her bridle. Then she rubbed down the mare and led her into her stall. She was about to get started on Sultan, when she heard her brother call out her name.

"Is something wrong, Ethan?" she asked, looking up at him.

"Anne brought me a slice of cake, but then Ma called for her, and she ran off without bringing it up to me," her brother said. "It's still on the ladder."

Molly stepped over to the ladder, picked up a bulky cloth napkin sitting on the middle rung, and climbed up to the hayloft. She crawled over to her brother and handed the napkin to him.

"Thanks," said Ethan, opening the napkin eagerly. He was about to take a bite of cake when he suddenly froze. He dropped the cake in the hay, pulled Molly down beside him, and slid forward so that he was lying flat. He put his finger to his lips as a signal to her to be quiet.

A second later, Molly heard the voices of Captain Foster and Lieutenant Hayden below them.

"Where did Corporal Hastings say he found the smugglers' ship?" Molly heard Captain Foster ask.

"A few miles up river," Lieutenant Hayden replied. "It was disguised as a British gunboat. There was a box of muskets on board, but no crew. It's unfortunate that they escaped, but we'll find them. Hastings was sure he knows where to locate their encampment."

Molly looked at her brother in horror. Foster and Hayden had been talking about Uncle William and his men!

"Right," said Captain Foster. "As soon as we're finished saddling up the horses, we'll round up a detachment of soldiers and leave for the smugglers' camp in half an hour."

Molly and Ethan lay still in the hay and waited. Finally, after what seemed to Molly to be hours instead of minutes, they heard the sound of the horses clip-clopping out of the barn. They lay there for a few more minutes. Then Molly got up.

"Uncle William has to be warned," she said desperately. "Pa has to take Sultan right now and warn him!" She started for the ladder, but Ethan pulled her back.

"Wait a minute, Molly," he said. "Didn't I hear Pa say he was going to shoe a redcoat's horse?" Molly nodded impatiently. "Well," Ethan continued, "if he leaves in a hurry, the redcoat might get suspicious."

He looked down at his broken leg and said bitterly,

"I'd go, but I can't. Anne hates horses, and Ma can't ride very well. Someone has to go, but who?"

Molly looked down at Sultan and thought hard. After a moment, she had made up her mind. She looked at her brother and said, "I'll go."

Race Against Time

"You?" Ethan said, staring at his sister in disbelief. "It's much too dangerous for you to ride all that way with an army of redcoats right behind you. Ma and Pa won't let you go."

"I'm not going to tell them," Molly said firmly. Then she added in a desperate tone, "There's no time to argue, Ethan. Someone has to warn Uncle William, and I'm the only one who can do it right now!"

Molly crawled away from him and scrambled down the ladder. She hurried over to Sultan and adjusted the stirrups to a shorter length. Then she untied him from the hitching post.

She was about to place her foot in the stirrup, when she thought of something. "Where is Uncle William's camp?" she called up to Ethan.

"It's twenty miles up the river," Ethan told her. "You follow the main road until you come to an abandoned red barn. Then you turn right and follow a dirt track that curves north, parallel with the river. You follow the river to a covered bridge. Across that bridge is a little island. That's where Uncle William and his men are camped. Can you remember all that?"

"Barn, track, river, bridge, island," Molly repeated, putting her left foot in the stirrup. "I've got it."

She took a deep breath, then pushed herself off the ground with her right foot. A second later, she was swinging her right leg over the saddle, just as she had done several days earlier when Richard Butler had helped her mount Sultan. But she had no time be pleased with herself. "It's up to you and me,'" she whispered, patting Sultan's neck.

She grasped the reins firmly, touched her feet lightly to Sultan's side, and steered him out of the barn. As she did, she heard Ethan call out softly, "Good luck, Molly. And be careful!"

As soon as they were out of the barn, Molly urged Sultan into a canter. As they passed the forge, Molly glimpsed her father looking out and noticed a startled expression on his face as she rode by.

When they reached the main road, Molly urged the Arabian into a gallop. Sultan took off like a shot, leaving her breathless. For a moment she was afraid that she was going to lose her seat, but then she leaned into him and began to sense the rhythm of his movement. She could feel the muscles of the beautiful Arabian rippling beneath her as they raced past trees, fields, and farms.

After riding a few miles, Molly spotted the red barn Ethan had told her about. She slowed Sultan to a canter and turned him onto the dirt track beside the barn. As she did, she glanced behind her anxiously to see if there were any redcoats following them. The road was empty, and she breathed a sigh of relief. "So far, so good," she murmured as she cantered Sultan down the track.

Just as Ethan had said, the track curved and then began to run north along the river. A mile further on it stopped, and Molly saw nothing but empty fields stretching before her. "If I keep following the river, I'll be all right," Molly reminded herself as she urged Sultan into a gallop once more.

They sped across the field for several miles until the ground underneath them started to grow wet and spongy. Molly knew they had reached the marshland

next to the river. Sultan slowed his pace only slightly as he splashed through shallow pools of water surrounded by marsh grass. Suddenly, in the distance, Molly saw a group of men standing by a grove of trees. She couldn't tell if they were redcoats or Americans, or even if they were soldiers. What if they are redcoats, she thought fearfully. She desperately looked for a way to circle the grove of trees, but there was a pond to the left of it, and on the right, the ground sloped steeply down to the river.

Then, as she rode closer to the group of men, she saw that some of them were wearing buckskin, like her Uncle William. Others were dressed in the blue jackets worn by many American soldiers. Maybe Uncle William has moved his camp down here, Molly thought, slowing Sultan to a canter and then to a walk. She hoped so. She was tired, and she was sure Sultan was tired, too.

The soldiers watched her as she rode up to them. One of them left the campfire he was tending and stepped up to her. He was a bearded man dressed in buckskins.

"Is Major William Randall here?" she asked the bearded soldier as she stopped the Arabian.

Instead of answering her question, he stroked his beard, and the soldier looked at her thoughtfully for a moment. Then he asked slowly, "And who might you be, miss?"

"I'm his niece, Molly Randall," Molly told him hurriedly. "I've ridden up here from Yorktown to warn him that the redcoats know about his smuggling and are coming after him and his men this very minute!"

The soldier raised his eyebrows in surprise as he listened to Molly. Then he shook his head. "Major Randall isn't here. His camp is six or seven miles further up the river. These men are a small detachment of American soldiers on their way to Williamsburg. But I thank you for the information, miss. Now we'll know to be on the lookout for a redcoat raiding party."

He began to stroke Sultan's neck, adding, "This is a fine animal you have here. But he looks tired. So do you, for that matter. I suggest you both stop a while and rest before going on. We can handle any redcoats who come our way."

Molly was tempted to take a rest, but she shook her head. "No, we have to find Uncle William right away," she told the soldier. "But I thank you, sir, I mean . . ."

"Captain," the soldier filled in for her. "Captain Eli Hamilton, late of the Richmond Militia, now with the American army. Well, young lady, if you're set upon continuing your journey now, I'd better tell you how to get on your way."

He pointed to a clearing in the grove of trees and said, "That clearing stretches on for about a mile. After that, you'll be back in open country."

Molly thanked him and spurred Sultan on. When they reached the clearing, she saw that it was wide enough to let her ride him at a gallop. The sun was just beginning to sink in the sky, and shafts of sunlight shot through the trees, making the leaves sparkle green and gold.

Despite Molly's worries about riding Sultan too hard, the Arabian didn't seem tired in the least. He galloped through the clearing at an even clip, and his breathing was regular and not labored.

Finally, through the trees, she glimpsed the open country. As she raced Sultan out of the clearing, she saw that up ahead there was a creek. Like the grove of trees, there was no way to go around it. She felt tears of frustration well up in her eyes as she slowed Sultan to a walk and then stopped him at the edge of the creek. "We'll never get across this creek," she wailed. "The water is moving too fast!"

Sultan tossed his head and nickered softly. Then, to Molly's surprise, he walked forward and began picking his way carefully along the rocks that led down to the creek. Molly held on tight as he stepped into the water up to his knees and slowly made his way across the current to the other side. He bounded up out of the water onto a small, rocky outcropping and continued walking.

"I always knew you were the most wonderful horse in the world," Molly whispered to him as she leaned over and stroked his neck. "And you just proved it!"

She let him walk for a while to dry off before urging him into a gallop again. They had ridden for several more miles when Molly saw a sight lit by the setting sun that made her eyes shine with joy. Straight ahead of them was a small inlet. And spanning the inlet was a covered bridge.

"We're almost there, Sultan," she exclaimed. "We just have a little way to go!"

As Molly cantered onto the covered bridge, she hoped that Sultan wouldn't become spooked by the darkness. But the Arabian kept going, his eyes fixed on the light at the end of the bridge, the sound of his hooves echoing off the wooden planks of the floor.

When they rode out of the bridge, Molly looked around eagerly for signs of her uncle's camp. She finally spotted campfires off to the right and saw a number of men in buckskins sitting around the fires eating and resting. She slowed Sultan to a walk and turned him in the direction of the campfires. As she was passing a stand of elm trees, two scruffy-looking men suddenly jumped down from the branches in front of her. They raised their muskets and shouted, "Halt! Who goes there?"

CHAPTER TEN

Safe at Last

Startled at the soldiers' sudden appearance, Sultan shied back a few paces. As Molly struggled to calm him, she stammered out, "I-I'm M-Molly Randall. Is my uncle, Major William Randall, here?"

The two soldiers lowered their muskets. "I'm sorry we frightened you and the horse, Miss," one of them said politely. "It's getting dark, and we couldn't see you properly from our lookout post in the trees. Your uncle is down by the river. I'll go and get him."

He hurried off. The other soldier turned and climbed back up the tree, his musket slung over his shoulder. A few minutes later, Molly saw her uncle striding toward her.

"For goodness sake, Molly, what are you doing here?" he asked, helping her down off Sultan.

Molly quickly told him about the redcoats' discovery of the smuggling ship and Captain Foster's and Lieutenant Hayden's plan to raid her uncle's camp. When she had finished telling him, he thought for a moment. Then he looked over at the men sitting around the campfires and called out, "Corporal Henshaw! Over here, on the double!"

A thin young soldier put down the plate he was holding, jumped up, and hurried over to them.

"Yes, Major?" he said, saluting smartly.

"Tell the men to pack up everything as fast as they can," Uncle William ordered. "We're moving five miles upriver to the safety zone.

"What's the safety zone?" Molly asked.

"It's an area north of here controlled by our allies, the French and German troops," Uncle William explained.

He took Molly's small hand and pressed it between his big ones. "Thank you for riding here to warn me, niece," he said, smiling warmly. "That was very brave of you."

"I couldn't have done it without Sultan," Molly told him. "He flew like the wind almost all the way. I used to be afraid to ride him, but not anymore. Now I can't even understand why I was ever afraid of him."

"Sometimes it takes a crisis for us to discover what we really can do when we have to," her uncle said. "You had to ride Sultan, so you did. Now you know how easy it is. It's as simple as that."

At that moment, Corporal Henshaw jogged over to them. He saluted to Uncle William and said, "The men are ready to go, sir."

"Right," Uncle William said. Then he turned to Molly. "It's much too dark and dangerous for you to return to Yorktown now. You and Sultan will have to ride with us to the safety zone and spend the night. I know you're worn out, and Sultan is, too, but do you think you could manage just a few more miles?"

She patted Sultan's neck. "After what Sultan and I just went through to get here, five more miles seems like nothing at all!"

She got back on Sultan, and her uncle mounted his horse. Then, with lanterns lighting the way, and Molly and Uncle William in the lead, the regiment rode across the bridge and headed north. After walking the horses for a mile, they came to the main road. There, they quickened the horses' pace to a canter.

Forty-five minutes later, they came to a farmhouse well-lit up by torches and guarded by French soldiers. One of the soldiers stepped up to Uncle William and spoke to him in French. Molly's eyes opened wide when she heard Uncle William answer him in the same language. The French soldier pointed to the left, in the direction of a small pasture, and ran back to the farmhouse.

"I didn't know you could speak French," Molly said as they turned the horses toward the pasture.

"I can't speak it very well," Uncle William admitted. "I learned a little French when I was fighting with the French troops last month, that's all. As I said before," he added with a grin, "you never know what you can do until you try."

When they reached the pasture, Uncle William ordered his men to dismount. Then he helped Molly down off Sultan. "Here's an extra halter and lead rope," he told her, reaching into his saddlebag.

"Thanks," Molly said, taking the halter and lead rope. "Do you think I could borrow a nosebag and a brush, too?"

"I'll see what I can do," her uncle promised.

Molly removed Sultan's saddle and bridle, and slipped the halter over his head. Then she led him over to a fence and tied him to one of the posts. Moments later, her uncle appeared with a pail of water, a full nosebag, and a brush. Molly let the Arabian take a long drink first. Then she brushed him

down to remove the sweat and dirt from his body.
When she had cleaned him up, she placed the
nosebag over his head. "Enjoy your supper, Sultan,"
she told him. "I wish I had an apple to give you, but
that will have to wait until we get home."

Just then, she felt her uncle take her arm. "Now
it's your turn," he said quietly. He gently steered her
over to a pile of blankets in front of a campfire. Molly
sat down, and her uncle draped another blanket
around her shoulders. Then he handed her a spoon
and a bowl filled with hot ham and bean soup. Molly
started to eat, but she soon began to feel sleepy. Her
eyelids drooped, and her head began to nod. Uncle
William took the spoon and bowl from her hands. She
lay down, curled up in her blanket, and was soon fast
asleep.

When Molly opened her eyes the next morning,
she had trouble remembering where she was. After a
moment, it all came back to her—the wild ride on
Sultan to warn Uncle William and their journey with
him to the safety zone. She sat up, shrugged off the
blanket, and looked over at Sultan, who was being
given water and a nosebag. Other soldiers were busy
feeding and grooming their own horses or eating their
breakfasts or drinking coffee from tin mugs.

One soldier picked up his saddlebag and walked over to Molly. He crouched down beside her, opened the saddlebag, and pulled out a big piece of salt pork and a flask of water. "This is the only breakfast we can offer you, I'm afraid," he said in an apologetic tone.

"That's all right," Molly said, smiling weakly. When he had gone, she wrinkled her nose at the salt pork, but she was too hungry not to eat it.

Suddenly, she drew her breath in sharply. A man was walking toward her dressed in the red-coated uniform of a British officer. Then, as the man came closer, she saw that it was her Uncle William.

"Surprised?" he said with a broad grin. "I captured a British captain during the battle and confiscated his uniform and hat. I thought they might come in handy someday."

"Why are you wearing it now?" Molly asked him.

"It's too dangerous for you to ride back to Yorktown by yourself, so I'm going with you," he told her. "This uniform will be a good disguise in case we should happen to run into real redcoats on the way. As soon as you saddle up Sultan, we'll go."

Half an hour later, Molly and her uncle set off at a canter down the main road toward Yorktown. "We'll keep to the road," Uncle William said to Molly. "It will be faster as well as easier on the horses. If we meet up with any redcoats, let me do all the talking."

Molly nodded to show that she understood. She was looking forward to getting home. Her dress and stockings were dirty and stained, and her hair was tangled and full of dust. She hoped there wouldn't be any redcoats on the road to delay them.

As they rode along, Molly was relieved to find that the only people they met were travelers like themselves.

The sun was high in the sky when Molly and Uncle William reached the Randalls' home. Molly rode Sultan into the yard in front of the forge, dismounted, and hurried toward the barn. "Ethan!" she called out as she stepped through the door. "I'm back!"

She looked up at the hayloft, and a moment later saw her brother grinning down at her. "Welcome back," he said. "Want to tell me all about it?"

"She might as well tell all of us about it now that we're all here," Molly heard her father's voice say behind her.

Molly turned and threw herself into Pa's arms. He hugged her tightly, whispering, "We're glad you're safe, daughter. We were very worried about you."

As Molly was hugging her mother next, she said, "But Ethan told you where I went, and why I was the one who had to go, didn't he?"

"Yes, but that didn't stop us from worrying, dear," Ma said, stroking her hair tenderly.

"Tell us what happened," Anne said, putting her arm around her sister.

So Molly told them all about her trip, from the time she and Sultan turned off the main road by the red barn to the moment she and Uncle William rode into the Randalls' yard.

"I'm very proud of you, Molly," Pa said, "even if you did cause us all a great deal of worry." He clapped his brother on the shoulder. "Thank you for bringing her back, Will."

"I think it's time we had our meal," Ma suggested gently. "You must be very hungry, Molly."

"I'm starving," Molly told her. "All I've had to eat today is some salt pork that tasted terrible." She looked at her uncle and grimaced. "Sorry, Uncle William."

"That's all right, Molly," her uncle said with a laugh. "I think it tastes terrible, too. But I'm a soldier, so I have to eat it."

After promising to bring Ethan his food later on, Molly went back to the house with her family. She changed her dress and combed her hair, and joined the others in the kitchen. There was roast chicken, sweet potatoes, stewed apples, and cornbread for their meal. Molly thought she had never tasted anything so delicious.

"I have some news," Anne said as they were eating. "It's about Richard Butler."

"Not now, dear," Ma said with a frown. "The news will keep."

Molly looked at her sister with an anxious expression. "What news?" she asked uneasily. "You have to tell me, Anne."

"Richard Butler is going to be hanged tomorrow morning," Anne said in a rush, relieved to get the news over with.

Molly dropped her fork on her plate with a clatter. "That's terrible," she cried. "Isn't there anything we can do to save him?"

"I'm afraid not," her father said quietly.

They all sat in silence for a moment. Then Uncle William grinned and said, "You know, I think there just might be a way to rescue Richard Butler. But I'll need a pen and some paper, John. And Molly, I'll need help from you and Sultan."

Molly Makes Up Her Mind

An hour later, a cart rolled down the road toward the town. Hitched to the cart was a beautiful dapple-gray Arabian horse with a silvery mane and tail. The cart was driven by what looked to be a young boy in a white shirt, breeches, and a tricorne hat. Trotting beside the wagon was a dignified-looking British officer.

The officer was Uncle William, and the boy was Molly. She was wearing clothes that had belonged to Ethan when he was about her age, and her hair was tied behind her with a ribbon. The horse was, of course, Sultan.

Molly held the reins firmly for fear that Sultan

116

would take off down the road at a gallop. But the Arabian responded to the touch of the reins as if he were used to pulling a cart every day.

"The jail is opposite Cornwallis's headquarters," Molly said as they rode into town. "What if he or one of the guards at his house sees us?"

Uncle William smiled confidently. "I don't think we have to worry about that, Molly. I happen to know that General Cornwallis always inspects his troops at this time in the afternoon. He leaves three or four men to guard his house, and they'll be too busy dicing or playing cards to question me too closely. Besides," he added, patting his jacket pocket. "I have a document here they wouldn't dare question."

But Molly couldn't help but feel nervous as they approached the jail. Uncle William had come up with a daring plan to save Richard Butler. Would it work?

When they reached the jailhouse, Molly pulled Sultan to a stop in front of it. She glanced over to the left and saw that Uncle William had been right about the redcoats guarding Cornwallis's house. There were four of them sitting on the stoop that led up to the house. They were taking turns throwing a pair of dice and calling out the numbers as they came up.

"Lucky seven," one of them drawled. "That's ninepence you owe me, Jack."

"You there," Uncle William barked so loudly that Molly flinched in her seat.

The soldiers looked up. When they saw Uncle William, they got to their feet quickly and snapped to attention.

"Who's the commanding officer here?" Uncle William snapped.

"I am, sir," one of the soldiers said, stepping forward and fumbling with his jacket as he tried to button it up. "Corporal Harmon, Sir."

"I am Captain Humphries," Uncle William said in clipped tones. "I have orders to remove the prisoner Richard Butler from this jail and take him to General Tarleton's headquarters across the river. The general wants to question Butler before he's hanged."

Uncle William took a paper out of his pocket and handed it to Corporal Harmon. "Here are my orders, signed by General Tarleton."

Molly knew that these orders had been written and the general's signature forged by Uncle William about an hour ago. She watched anxiously as the corporal took the paper, unfolded it, and looked at it. He pursed his lips and knit his brow as he peered at the paper closely. Molly felt her heart sink. She was sure the corporal knew that the paper was a forgery and that he wasn't going to let Mr. Butler go.

But after a moment, he nodded and turned to his men. "Private Parker, go fetch the prisoner," he ordered. Then he handed the paper back to Uncle William. Molly's uncle tucked the paper into his pocket.

A few minutes later, the door of the jailhouse opened, and Molly saw Richard Butler step outside, his hands tied behind his back. The bright sunshine made him blink. He was in his shirtsleeves, and Molly noticed that his neckcloth was rumpled and torn.

"Put him in the cart," Uncle William ordered. The private gripped Mr. Butler's arm and pushed him over to the cart. Mr. Butler glanced at Molly and Sultan, then stepped up into the cart and sat on the floor.

Uncle William turned to Corporal Harmon and said coldly, "I am shocked to see a soldier in His Majesty's army dressed in such a sloppy fashion. I'll have to report this to General Cornwallis. Meanwhile, button up your jacket at once, Corporal!"

Corporal Harmon turned red and hastily did as he was ordered. Molly stifled a giggle.

"Right," said Uncle William. "We'll be off." Molly spoke to Sultan, and the Arabian stepped forward. She pulled on the left rein, and Sultan turned.

When they were a safe distance away from the jail, Richard Butler said, "I thank you both from the bottom of my heart. If you hadn't tricked them, it would have been the end of me. But how did you come to be in Yorktown, Major Randall?"

Molly and Uncle William took turns explaining to him how Molly had ridden Sultan to warn her uncle, and what had happened after that.

"So I have you to thank for helping to save my life, Molly," Mr. Butler said warmly. "I think you are the bravest girl I know."

Molly glowed with pride. But she knew that someone else deserved credit, too. "It wasn't just me, Mr. Butler," she told him. "I couldn't have done it without Sultan. If he hadn't stepped into the creek on his own, I would never have reached Uncle William's camp."

Molly's parents were waiting for them outside the barn when they arrived. Molly stopped the cart, jumped down, and ran over to hug them. "We did it!" she exclaimed.

"Congratulations, daughter," Pa said with a smile. "And you, too, Will."

"Thanks, John," Molly's uncle said as he took out a knife and cut the rope binding Richard Butler's hands. "But right now, I'm still worried about you, Mr. Butler. It's not safe for you to stay in Yorktown."

"I was hoping you'd take me with you, Major," Mr.

Butler said, rubbing his wrists where the rope had cut into them. "I'd like to join the American army, officially this time."

Uncle William smiled at him. "I think that can be arranged, Mr. Butler," he said, slapping him on the back.

"But first I'll need to find a horse," Mr. Butler told him.

Molly stared at him in surprise. "What about Sultan?"

Mr. Butler smiled down at her. "Well, I had thought of leaving Sultan with you until the war is over. I know you'll take good care of him, Molly."

Molly felt a rush of joy. Sultan could stay here, and she could ride him every day. She stepped over to the Arabian and stood there looking at him, her eyes shining. Then, as she gazed at him, she suddenly felt tears welling up in her eyes. She knew what she had to do.

She turned to Richard Butler. "I can't keep him, Mr. Butler," she said, trying to keep her voice from trembling. "We had some wonderful adventures together, but he belongs with you. You'll need him in the army."

"Are you sure, Molly?" Mr. Butler said quietly.

Molly gulped and nodded. "I'm sure."

She managed to hold back her tears until Sultan was saddled and Mr. Butler was on his back. Then, with tears streaming down her face, she put her arms around the Arabian's neck. "Good-bye, Sultan," she whispered. "I'll miss you."

"I'll bring him back safe and sound," Mr. Butler told her. "That's a promise."

Molly stepped away and watched as Richard Butler and Uncle William rode out of the yard. Her father came up to her and put his arm around her shoulders. "That was a very grown-up decision you made just now," Pa said softly. "Ma and I are very proud of you."

Molly tried to smile, but she was feeling very sad. Then, she heard Flora whinny. She turned and saw Flora in the pasture, tossing her head, demanding attention.

Molly laughed and brushed the tears from her eyes. "You act like such a baby sometimes," she told Flora as she walked over to the mare and gave her a big hug.

With her arms around Flora's neck, Molly gazed at Sultan cantering up the road, his tail carried proudly. Molly thought of all the wonderful rides she and Sultan would have after the war was over and Richard Butler brought him safely home.

FACTS
ABOUT THE BREED

You probably know a lot about Arabians from reading this book. Here are some more interesting facts about this ancient and beautiful breed.

∩ Arabians generally stand between 14.1 and 15.1 hands. Instead of using feet and inches, all horses are measured in hands. A hand is equal to four inches.

∩ Pure-bred Arabians often have black skin, while their coats may be of any color. Their dark skin shines through around the eyes and makes the horse look as if it is wearing eyeliner.

∩ Arabians have silky manes and tails and arched necks. The muzzle is smaller than that of most breeds. Some people say that the Arabian's snout is so delicate it could drink from a teacup.

∩ The Arabian's most prominent characteristic is its dished face. The Arabian, in profile, has a face that curves inward below the eyes.

∩ Arabians are spirited horses. They like to run and often do so with their lovely tails held up behind them like banners. One legend has it that in ancient times, an Arabian rider tore off his cloak while escaping from an enemy. After he had arrived safely back at camp, he found his cloak hanging on the upraised tail of his mare.

∩ The Arabian, a small and tough horse, is the oldest breed. While their very beginnings are uncertain, we do know that thousands of years ago the Bedu tribes of the Arabian desert carefully bred their horses for stamina and beauty.

∩ These ancestors of today's horses were treated like one of the family. They even slept in the same tent with their owners. Perhaps this early closeness with people accounts for the friendly disposition of the Arabian today.

∩ Arabians have played an important role in history. In the seventh and eighth centuries, Arabian horses helped Muslim armies to occupy large areas of Europe and Asia.

∩ Napoleon, emperor of the French (1804-15), rode a gray Arabian stallion named Marengo. Although Marengo was wounded eight times in his career as a war horse, he carried Napoleon safely through many battles. Marengo was captured and taken to England after the battle of Waterloo. After he died, at 38 years of age, his skeleton was put on display at the National Army Museum.

∩ During colonial times, Arabians were among the first horses to be brought to America. In fact, George Washington's horse, Magnolia, was an Arabian.

∩ Arabians have been used as the foundations for several other breeds. Thoroughbreds, famous for their great racing speed, were developed in the eighteenth century from three Arabian stallions—the Byerly Turk, the Godolphin Arabian, and the Darley Arabian.

∩ Arabians have also been used to develop and improve other breeds, including the Colorado Ranger, the American Shetland, and even the heavy Percheron. Today almost all riding horses have some Arabian ancestry.

∩ Arabians and part Arabians are bred in Australia, France, England, Spain, Poland, Austria, Germany, the United States, the United Arab Emirates, Jordan, and other countries all over the world. Two famous Arab breeding farms, or studs, are in Hungary. Babolna is known for its Shagya Arab, which was used as a mount for the Hungarian cavalry. The Gidran Arab, which is bigger than a pure-blood Arabian, comes from Mezohegyes.

∩ In the United States, Arabians have become such popular pleasure horses that there now are more Arabians in America than there are in all of the Arab countries.

∩ While Arabians are best known for their stamina (they can travel long distances over rough terrain), they are truly all-purpose horses. Today Arabians compete in the dressage ring. They win ribbons in hunter classes. They even trot along dusty paths on western trail rides much as their ancestors did crossing the deserts of ancient Arabia.